Half

Also by Sharon Harrigan

Playing with Dynamite: A Memoir

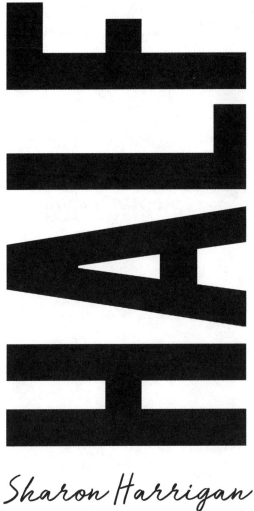

HALF

Sharon Harrigan

The University of Wisconsin Press

Publication of this book has been made possible,
in part, through support from the **Brittingham Trust.**

The University of Wisconsin Press
728 State Street, Suite 443
Madison, Wisconsin 53706
uwpress.wisc.edu

Gray's Inn House, 127 Clerkenwell Road
London EC1R 5DB, United Kingdom
eurospanbookstore.com

Printed in the United States of America

This book may be available in a digital edition.

Library of Congress Cataloging-in-Publication Data

Names: Harrigan, Sharon, 1967- author.
Title: Half / Sharon Harrigan.
Description: Madison, Wisconsin: The University of Wisconsin Press, [2020]
Identifiers: LCCN 2019050460 | ISBN 9780299328542 (paperback)
Subjects: LCSH: Identical twins—Fiction. | LCGFT: Fiction. | Novels.
Classification: LCC PS3608.A78158 H35 2020 | DDC 813/.6—dc23
LC record available at https://lccn.loc.gov/2019050460

To
James,
of course

Half

Prologue

(Christmas, 2030)

We wedged Mom between us. Her sharp hips bore into ours as we sat on the hard pew. She nodded toward the blizzard raging on the other side of the stained glass and said, "It's your dad."

"He's making it snow?" As identical twins, we spoke in unison. People responded to us, at least, as if we did.

Mom chewed her index finger and kept quiet. We took that as a yes. Apparently, she was still claiming Dad controlled everything and the weather, even though we had just flown in for his funeral. "Preposterous," we told each other with our shoulders and palms. Whether we meant the weather or the funeral, we didn't say.

In the twelve years since we had moved away, monster storms had become the norm. Planes were no longer even grounded for them.

The eulogies droned on. Ms. Rosen, our fourth-grade teacher, swished up to the pulpit, butterfly tattoos sagging under the stretched skin on her now-ample arms, charm bracelet tinkling. She praised Dad and God in the same sentence.

Next came Wild Pete, Dad's old buddy from his days of leading hunting tours in Alaska, his squirrelly mustache muffling a gruff voice. He told the origin story of Dad's nickname, Moose. We had heard tales about Pete all our lives but had secretly suspected he wasn't real.

Our childhood best friends described a man whose beard never grayed, whose shot never missed, who was "always there." *Always where?* we asked, only in our heads, in a voice that sounded more like the snarky teens we had been than the thirty-year-old moms we were now.

We had prepared nothing. Mom could barely stand up, let alone speak, but we, the daughters, should have represented the family. That's what everyone's eyes on us said. A young man with a slender purple tie and a square of hair on his flinty chin glared from the other side of the aisle.

Mom sagged against the wooden pew. Her face, already slim from a lifetime of dieting, turned gaunt. Her still-dark hair—so thick that even in middle age she had enough to pile it high, goddess style, on her head—seemed to thin by the minute. A tiny lily tattoo wilted on the back of her neck. Even the beauty mark above her lip shrank.

Our five-year-old sons, clutching plush hedgehogs and snapping their bow ties, sat on our other sides. Next to them, our husbands, lost in an incense fog. Tears would have been a relief, but we dammed them back.

"Marco." We said it so low it might have been telepathy.

"Polo," came our reply, barely audible.

We reached over Mom to knock knuckles on each other's thighs. We fingered the single earring we each wore, a diamond stud. As long as we shared this pair, these secret codes, we thought we couldn't fall apart.

At the reception, Wild Pete almost tore off our hands, pretending to shake them. Breath thick with chaw, he said, "You're the ones who killed him."

We slipped from Pete's grip, pushed outside, and leaned against the wall near the church basement steps, eyelashes weighted with snow.

"We didn't," we said.

Then, "We did."

"How could he say such a thing?"

"You mean, how could he know?"

We had to hold each other's coats to keep from falling with the snow. Gusts swirled at our ankles, and snow hooped around our hips. We braced against the scratchy brick, gripping.

"Why did we do it?" we asked each other.

"Because of what he did to us. Every year of our lives."

We couldn't live with ourselves if we thought we had killed an innocent man. A jury of two, we had to decide if Dad deserved what we had done to him. The only evidence to review was our childhood.

We clutched each other's hands for heat, our bodies so close we could imagine we were attached—"Siamese"—

the way we had pretended to be so long ago. Spines in fetal curve, we rewound the tape of our lives in our heads, starting back at the age our own boys were now.

"Remember?" we said.

We had never meant to hurt anyone.

Part One

1

*W*e wanted to crawl back in time. Even then. We were only five, but that wasn't young enough.

The more we played this game—hovering outside our parents' door after dinner, trying to hear their mysterious bedroom sounds while pretending we didn't—the more we wanted to be babies again. Or even to slip back into our mother's belly, the way we slid into her bed those nights when Dad was away on a hunting trip.

"I'm half years old," we said. "How old are you?"

"I'm half, too."

At first we meant we had been alive six months, just half a year. Later, half no longer stood for anything. Half empty, half full.

We babbled and baby-talked, the way our own children do now when they don't want us to understand. Our friend Nevaeh had a baby brother, and he was always sucking at his mother's breast, so we knew milk was food, milk was love.

We were twin girls, born in 2000, the year of the Golden Dragon. Our dark bangs hung crooked, cut with the blunt scissors sometimes used for discipline. We listened through the hollow-core door as the mattress squeaked, wondering why our parents were jumping on the bed. They never let us.

We were locked out of the one private room in the house. We wanted to walk in on them now, the way we liked to sneak in on Mom when she tried to escape from us in the bath, slinky and slippery as a mermaid. But even if the door hadn't been locked, we wouldn't have dared, not with Dad in there. He was a lion escaped from the zoo. He could hunt us down and eat us in our sleep. He roared, and all his subjects scattered. He was king.

"I'm so little I can't walk," we said, floundering on our bellies, flapping our arms.

We said, "I can't even talk," then "You're talking now," and "No, I'm not. You're reading my mind."

As identical twins, we had our own identical language. We understood each other's taps and scraps of song, our code for "Ignore the sounds behind the door." We pressed noses to knees, legs bent crisscross applesauce on the dirt-brown shag, which meant: "We can't do anything to help her, anyway. We're too little."

We lay on top of each other, like the puppies we saw at the pet store. Our dog, Rex, had to live outside, and we weren't allowed to snuggle him in the house the way we were nuzzling each other now. We wanted to buy him a sister or brother from the pound, the way we had once thought our parents bought us from the hospital, two for one, on double-coupon day.

The bouncing on the bed became a pounding beat. It shook the floor and squeaked like something breaking. "Earthquake," we said. "Quicksand." We meant "he's big and she's small." She was so thin she could have slipped through the metal bars of a cage. If she wanted to.

We pretended we were in a crib and couldn't climb out. We made believe we were still at the hospital after being born and there was some hope another family might take us by mistake, the way the cashier sometimes gave Mom the wrong cigarettes at Lucky Seven.

Mom made animal noises on the other side of the door, dog shrieks, worse than our whimpers when Dad punished us for breaking a glass or sharing a secret. We wanted to save her but were stranded on an island the size of this hallway, and if we stepped out we would drown.

We half-wanted to open the door. We leaned into it so we could feel the vibrations of Mom's cries.

We pressed so hard, our heads pushed the door in, and we fell forward. But no, it was Dad hovering over us, wearing only boxer shorts, his huge hairy hand on the knob. He was on his way to the bathroom. "Kids!" he yelled, stepping on and over us, his bare foot catching our footed pajamas, "Get to bed!"

To Mom he said, "Don't you teach these girls about privacy? What about manners?"

We could see through the legs of his boxer shorts as we lay on the floor facing up. "It's not her fault," we almost said. We didn't want him to make her squeal again with what we couldn't have imagined was pleasure. But we didn't talk back.

Mom pulled the covers over her naked breasts. She flicked her fingers to shoo us away, so we scampered off to our room.

"No fair! Daddy gets milk," we said to each other after crawling into our twin beds and pulling rubber ducky blankets up to our chins. "Milk is for babies!"

We dreamed a kiss on our foreheads, and, like magic, Mom appeared between us, dressed again in her T-shirt and jeans. "Good night, sweets!" she said.

"Why were you naked?" What we wouldn't say, what we didn't dare, was, "What did he do to make you scream?"

"Your dad likes me that way," she said, turning red. She seemed unhurt, not like Rex when he had made the same sounds she had made in bed.

"We like you that way, too," we said, and stretched our arms to pull her under the covers.

"You're way too old for that." She tore herself from us, far out of reach. "You're my two big kids. My two eyes and ears. My too, too much."

We could see her breasts shining through her T-shirt as bright as the moon in the dark of our room. We imagined her nursing us as we lay in the crook of each arm, safe on her lap, skin touching skin.

"Enough." And when she pressed a finger over her lips, Dad appeared like a ghost in the doorway.

"Why are you babying them?" he said. Then they vanished, the room dark and quiet till we heard their bedroom door close again.

"Why does the sun rise every morning?" we asked.

We answered in a fake Mom voice: "Because your dad likes it that way."

"Why does it get so cold every winter we freeze our butts off?"

"Because our butts are too big?"

"No, because your dad likes it that way."

"Why is the sky blue? Why does the devil have horns? Why does fire burn?"

"Because your dad likes it that way."

We spread our palms on our foreheads, over Mom's kiss so it seeped through our skin to those places—in our ribs or hips, ears or thighs—where Dad had kicked us on the floor. Our pale skin would swell like purple gumdrops the next day, and Mom would say, "No short shorts for you."

Dad's words echoed in our heads: "Why do you make me teach you the same lesson over and over again? Why didn't you go to bed after dinner like I told you to?"

We couldn't answer why we didn't learn our lessons. Why we didn't pick up dirty clothes, why we forgot to call him sir. Why did deer run into traffic? Bugs fly into light bulbs?

We lay in the beds we had made for ourselves, half

awake, half asleep. Half innocent, half guilty, half understanding everything he said.

Dad taught us other lessons, too. How to dog paddle,
throw a snowball, and fry a perfect egg. He taught us Arabic
words he had picked up in the army, little shrapnel sounds,
sharp and rapid fire. But we preferred soft baby talk, words
hushed the way we were on hunting trips with him.

He said he would teach us how to be as quiet as a dead
man. How to hold our tongues and breath and bladders.
How to disappear into the forest, become the wind, and
wait for prey.

One day Dad threw Rex into the covered truck bed
with us and drove for hours, till the factory smoke disappeared and the asphalt roads turned to dirt. Dad wedged
the brown truck we called the Bull between two No Trespassing signs. We flung open the doors and spilled into
the woods. Rex shot ahead, sniffing rabbits out of holes,
while we girls hauled ammo and water. The leaves smelled
like belly button fuzz and soggy cereal. Our seedling legs
bent in the wind, but we tried to keep up with the strides
of Dad's tree trunk thighs.

We wanted to inherit his speed, so we raced to catch
up, our three steps barely big as one of his. In the country,
his arms and feet and shoulders expanded. Even his beard.

Everyone called him Moose. Lou became Loose when he left home, he explained. Between dropping out of school and becoming our dad was a year in Alaska, when his buddies changed the *L* to *M*. Moose stuck. It fit like skin.

"Can we be Moose, too?" we asked. "Moose Jr.?" It never occurred to us that he would say "junior" was only for boys.

"I can't call you two the same," Dad said. "You confuse everyone enough already."

"So who gets it?"

"Whoever catches me."

By the time we realized what we were supposed to do, he had already bolted out of sight. Phlegm choked our throats. We sped after him, through bittersweet and green briars, slipping on leaves and flinging the brambles out of our path and into each other's thin skin.

One of us, fleeter of foot, could have won—if the other hadn't pulled her back. We averaged ourselves so much, almost no one knew the mismatch of our speeds, our muscles, our voices, our minds.

We might have caught him, had we not been holding hands. His feet flashed so fast, all we saw in his place was lightning in the cloudless sky. That's how he made the weather, we figured. Maybe he could teach us, too, if we ever found him again.

He was gone.

Maybe we would have to live in the forest and eat mushrooms. Maybe we would accidentally eat a poison one and die. If we weren't hunted down first.

The tears we sucked in thickened to syrup behind our eyes. Our blood ran cold as sap; our feet took root. When we opened our mouths to yell, only wind came out.

We were all alone.

Except for the mountain lions and bears—which sounded exactly like our heartbeats. To hide from predators, we climbed a tree and waited in its crook. We didn't talk or pee. Our breath came soundless, through our skin.

Quiet as a dead man.

Dad finally returned. How long had it been? Had we turned into trees?

Rex ran at Dad's heels. Two rabbits with broken necks dangled from Dad's hands. Quick, before he left again, we parachuted from the tree into his arms.

"You vanished," he said.

We folded, heads to chests, bellies to knees. He had told us to catch him, and we failed.

He fingered the metal on his belt. We knew what that meant, and we bristled. Could we make his belt vanish, too, the way we just had—but never come back?

"I said I'd teach you to disappear into the woods," he said. "And you learned. Took me a whole year in the army before I knew as much as I just taught you." Our favorite chocolate bars appeared in his palms, then slipped into our pockets—one with peanuts, one plain. Everyone else always gave us the same.

He slapped our backs, the way he hit his buddies when he told a dirty joke. He said he would make us rabbit coats, that he had been saving the pelts for us. We would be the envy of our kindergarten class.

He didn't pull off his belt and crook us over his knees. Not yet, at least. We never knew when he would. Instead, he took out his pocketknife. "Now let me teach you how to clean these buggers up."

He lay the rabbits down on moss. Hands on ours, he helped us slit our dinner, throat to tail. We pushed back the rusty taste in our mouths, locking teeth. The animals' insides spilled out. And—as soon as we found a bush to hide behind, pretending to pee—so did ours.

When we got mad at Dad, we said his secret name, only to each other. Lou became Loooo became Ewwww—what we called a slimy brown banana, on sale and way past expiration. "Call me sir," Dad said when he was mad at *us*.

When Mom called Dad "dear," we heard "deer." We heard "skin" milk instead of "skim." From a skinny cow? We said "melk" instead of milk, the Michigan way.

Dad called Mom her real name, Sera, only when he yelled. Mostly, he said "babe," though drunk, he would call her Hera. "My goddess." And if anyone asked, he would explain, "It's a Greek joke. My folks come from Athens." But from the other side of his bedroom door, we heard him grunt, all serious in worship of her, "Oh god oh god oh god."

We girls were named for famous twins. Artis for the hunter Artemis, Dad reminded us when we whimpered that the gear he made us carry was so heavy it hurt. Paula for Apollo, famous for playing the lute. "I'll make you musicians," he said, "if I have to kill you first."

Once we started school, Mom tried to return to the bank job she had had before we were born, but most of the tellers were gone. Her old boss said it was cheaper to use ATMs. Robots, we called them.

So Mom started a business. Sunflower Daycare, run from home. She painted the door with giant petals and silkscreened T-shirts so yellow they almost smelled like mustard.

For our birthday that year, Dad taught us to strum. "Only electricity you need," he said, "is the kind you make yourself." We begged him to let us wear our frou-frou flowered skirts. "It's a holiday." He gave in, but dressed the same as always himself: baggy jeans and a denim shirt with metal snaps, red high-tops and a skeleton stud in one ear. He shook his fingers, so we did, too. "Feel the buzz?" He showed us how to shuffle our soles on the storm-colored concrete, build up a spark, then give the guitar a shock. Zing went the strings, charring our nails.

He showed us how to play by ear, to hear our bellies fill with air, then make our fingers mimic the sun and clouds and wind. We listened to Rex chase squirrels, then made the strings squeal. We matched the sounds of spiderwebs squeaking in the armpits of doors.

Dad told us to peel off our socks and feel the vibrations on the cold, bare basement floor as we plucked. Our big toes swelled with the sound that echoed against unfinished walls the color of soot. Our fingers turned to meat, our bones creaked. He made us play through the pain after our skin cracked and bled. We thought every dad did.

"If we used picks," he said, "we wouldn't build up calluses."

The lesson done, he told us to figure out how to play Happy Birthday on our own. We thought every kid could learn a song in an afternoon, too.

"And then?" we asked.

His eyes grew round as cakes. "You'll get a present."

If we didn't do what he said, it would be just like any other day. But with bloody thumbs.

"Happy birthday to us," we sang along as we picked out the notes, wrong then wrong then finally right. One of us learned, then taught the other one how.

We mounted the stairs on frozen toes. "Now we're ready for our present," we told Dad.

He pointed with his beard. "You got it in your hands."

"The guitar? It's not a toy."

"Damn right. What you got is an antique."

"All our friends get toys."

He shook his head, and the room darkened. We heard the clink of his nails on the metal of his belt buckle. So we shut our mouths, and his hands went silent, too.

Haley and Nevaeh and Bo got thumb-size talking dolls and motorized hamsters for their birthdays. They got game systems that fit in their pockets and dolls that looked exactly like them. Most of all we wanted toy robots that would sing us to sleep when Mom was stuck in her room with Dad, behind the closed door, making sounds we thought we would never try to copy on the guitar.

We fished Rex's ball out of his house and used the guitar as a racket. We took turns throwing and whacking, plinking the strings so much Dad heard and stormed out.

He grabbed our hair at the scalp, yanking hard enough to give us bald spots. If chickens were plucked alive, their skin would sting like this. They would peck holes in his hand, but what could we do? Our mouths were made soft. "Didn't I tell you it's not a toy? Why do you make me teach you things the hard way?"

Why do rabbits run out of their holes? we asked each other with our hands, smoothing our hair. Why did Rex jump on the kitchen table whenever we opened the back door and accidentally let him in? Why had we tried to break the guitar when we could feel in our fingers that we were born to carry it everywhere, that it was part of us, like an extra arm?

Now his belt did come out. But we didn't want to remember what happened after that.

Our Papu died when we were five. We didn't know how. We didn't know why. We didn't know much.

But we overheard Ya-Ya, Dad's mom, whisper, "I always knew you'd kill him." She was talking to Dad, who sat, with her and Mom and us, in the front pew at the funeral. A black lace veil hung over her face, and her voice was soft, but we could read her lips, while everyone else closed their eyes for prayer.

We stared at her shiny black pumps, the kind of shoes our teachers wore. You could see your face in them if you looked close enough. Dad's lace-ups were scuffed. Mom's high-heeled sandals showed off nail polish the color of bruises.

We weren't supposed to peek or eavesdrop. Ya-Ya liked to say, "Keep your nose out of it."

But it was too late. Our eyes and ears and noses had minds all their own. There was no way to un-know that Dad had killed. And could again.

Our black vampire dresses itched against the unforgiving wooden pew. Moldy lettuce smells and old lady perfume mixed with monster-movie organ music.

We wanted to cry for Papu, but we were too big. How often had we heard that only babies cry? Old people, too. Ya-Ya's face reddened like a Swedish Fish.

We wanted to ask why people had to die. We had never known anyone who had before. Why, why, why? We wanted to ask every question that had ever been invented, we wanted to do every search that was ever done on the internet, but our mouths wouldn't move. Our teeth clamped tight. We couldn't open up, even to breathe. We had to sniffle through our nostrils. The air thickened with snot.

The priest said we would see Papu again in heaven, but he didn't say when. Tomorrow? This winter? If he was an angel now, would we find him in the snow? Could we lie on the ground and flap our arms and legs in the fluffy flakes and become angels, too? We wanted to ask Mom, and if she didn't know, we wanted her to ask a teacher.

"He's in a better place." The priest ruffled his robes while lifting his head to the sky. "Up there."

On the ceiling? In the clouds?

2

We still didn't know. Frosty breath clouded our eyes.
We strummed the air, playing snow guitar, the way he had taught us.

No. We taught ourselves.

We thumbed the snaps on our coats and the buttons on our bellies, a reflex, trying to connect. But we couldn't feel a thing, our puffy down like a layer of bear on our skin.

Those chocolate bars still swished in our gut, too sweet. Too different?

Yes.

He was always trying to keep us separate, even then.

We slid closer together across the brick wall, letting it shelter us from the storm. He taught us how to survive the elements.

And how to kill.

Stained light through church windows beckoned us inside to rejoin our kin. To thaw, to hide, to talk? We couldn't decide.

What could we tell them? What did we know? The snow blew sideways, so we had to lean our heads on each other's shoulders and close our eyes to invite the glimmers in.

3

*D*ad scooped us out of bed, still wrapped in rubber
ducky quilts, and carried us out to the Bull. His
beard reeked of coffee and bacon, his breath a whiff of
forest fire. He stacked our hats and coats and gloves next
to us in the covered flatbed and headed up the mitten of
Michigan. We leaned against the windows in lawn chairs,
facing each other, feet touching, Rex taking turns napping
in each of our laps.

"We'll let your mom sleep," Dad shouted from the
front seat. "When she wakes up, we'll tell her winter's
over."

"Is it?"

"You want it to be?" He honked on the empty road,
and the sun came up. Then he blasted the radio and sang
along.

Who else had a dad who let them decide? Who else
lived with the boss of the world?

We studied all the holidays in first grade. There was
one Easter Bunny, one Santa Claus, and one Groundhog.
We weren't surprised Dad knew exactly where he lived.

We also knew The Groundhog didn't know anything

Dad hadn't already figured out. He knew we stuffed our smelly socks under the bed instead of cleaning our room. That we lied when we said we would never do it again. He could make hail pelt down in the middle of a picnic.

The Bull climbed the interstate. We crunched granola bars and sucked juice out of boxes. We shouted out the highway exits till we came to ours.

Finally we slid to a stop, Rex cannonballed out, Dad hauled a backpack as big as a motorhome over his shoulders, and we tumbled off our seats, the scratchy nylon whistling when we rubbed it the wrong way. We brushed off specks of sleep. Our laps chilled with sweat where Rex had slept.

We pulled snowpants, coats, and furry boots over our pajamas and climbed the steps to a deer blind that made us invisible. We squabbled over binoculars and squinted so hard we said we could see underground. No sign of The Groundhog yet, or anything else. All the houses and people must have disappeared. Or they were invisible, too.

Dad wore his winter uniform: flannel, jeans, and fleece. No coat. Just a cap flipped back. "Wake up, Groundhog, and smell the gunpowder." He clicked the safety off his rifle. He always brought it with him into the woods, whether he meant to use it or not. It was his right, he would say, if someone asked. But no one dared.

"He won't shoot it, will he?" We didn't ask him directly. There's a time for questions and a time for guns. Dad taught us that. Rex cocked his ears and tried to bolt. Dad clutched his collar till he choked.

"Come on," Dad whispered, not loud enough for The Groundhog to hear and run away. "You think you're a bear? You ain't nothing but a fat-ass squirrel."

We crouched to keep warm. "Don't move," Dad said, as if we could. We were frozen still. At least we weren't at school, looping letters till our hands ached. If only those kids knew we could change the seasons without lifting a finger.

"Cold enough?" Dad asked.

Every bump on our skin said yes. Dad rubbed our arms and told us about the time he spent with Wild Pete up in Alaska. That year he rode moose, he said, steering with their antlers. Leading hunting tours into the woods where no cars dared. Catching bears in net bags, making them yowl before setting them free. Plucking feathers from pheasants in flight. Making cougars scatter like chipmunks. Trekking up the side of McKinley, no rope, no help, climbing like an animal, sniffing the way. No more implausible than Sunday school stories we heard at Ya-Ya's church.

From his monster pack, Dad whipped out thermoses and flasks, hot chocolate and throat-burning whiskey, sandwich bags of homemade jerky. He pulled out gloves without fingers, whistles without sound. Orange caps to keep us from shooting each other by mistake. Our hair hung down from the hats in double ponytails like icicle lights.

He brought out little gifts from his Alaskan life: a pocketknife inlaid with mother-of-pearl, a peacock feather— or was it from a phoenix? A narwhal tusk, he said, but we saw a unicorn. And fairy wings. He said they came from hummingbirds.

From his Santa sack emerged hand warmers and rocks so hot they must have come from the core of the Earth, the middle part we had learned about in school. Then beaver fur to wrap around our necks, coin-size whale blubber to savor like candy, wolf teeth to chew through childish thoughts, Dad said.

The wind blew upside-down, across the field and up to the bitter winter sky, but it didn't chill us. Anymore.

We were a pile of fur. We forgot why we were there. We were lost in Alaska.

And then he appeared, The Groundhog himself. "Look!" Dad said, sliding the binoculars over.

"Does he see his shadow and slink back into his hole? Or is he through sleeping?" Dad really meant: *Whatever you want him to do, he'll do it.*

Spring or a lingering winter? We weren't sure what we wanted anymore. Six more weeks of winter didn't sound so bad. If it was like Alaska, we would take it. We would ride on moose and fly on hummingbirds' wings.

But all the kids at school would hate us. You must be cold-blooded if you don't like spring, they would say. They would ask us, Whose side are you on?

We wanted to drink flasks of hot chocolate mixed with whiskey and eat homemade jerky. We wanted to stay in this deer blind with Dad until *next* Groundhog Day.

"Is he done sleeping?" The blind shook with the stomp of Dad's big foot.

We heard the words start to form, then stop, not yet in our throats but in the spaces behind our eyes. The open palm of the *Y* in yes, then the skin-pricking tips of the *N* in no. We had seconds to answer before the earth would open up and we would be sucked in. Seconds to decide. Should spring start now?

Dad grabbed our hands and planted them deep in the back of his neck, the warmest spot this side of the core of the Earth.

Finally, we said, "Yes."

Then it was over. Dad dropped our hands and the sun streamed down. The Groundhog hadn't seen his shadow. "Yes." We had said yes. The snow began to melt in our mouths before the whole word was out. Frost turned to slush. We found ourselves standing in puddles.

Dad loosed Rex, who chased all the animals from their holes. Bang bang bang! Dad shot into the air, the way he did on New Year's Eve. "Happy New Year!" we yelled, as if it were, pretending everything was starting fresh.

The rifle bucked, convulsing the whole blind. Its fire warmed our fingertips, our bodies, and our heads.

What was Dad shooting way up in the air? Heaven? Was that where Alaska was? Papu, too?

It was cold out there, but we were growing thicker skin. Calluses everywhere.

We pressed a finger on our nose, then chin, which was how we told each other not to tell anyone. We still haven't. Even we forgot, until now.

Why invite others to laugh? They wouldn't believe Dad let us change the weather. They would say we lied if we told them he taught us how to wish a thing and make it so.

Did it matter? We saw with our own eyes. We could see everything out there, even our steamy breath, our sticky sweat. We whooped and walloped along with the dog.

4

That was the year of our epic flu. No wonder—we had lingered so long in the punishing cold. Just as we were doing now, letting the chill numb our lips so much we could barely speak.

Which was perhaps the point. We could argue better with our elbows and knees, those sharpest of bones.

Sometimes he spent all morning before his shift fluffing up our pillows and singing us to sleep. Other times he called us babies for complaining of pain. We could disagree about the way he had nursed us back into the thick of life, boiled marrow for broth, cooled our foreheads with a stern glare, steamed up the room with his hot temper so our chests would clear. How he was two different dads, depending on the day and the person you asked.

Like Granny?

Exactly.

5

"Hello?" we said in stereo, then placed the cordless land-line where we both could hear. Hair banded into bushy tails, we lit like squirrels on a wire. Flame-resistant nightgowns scratched our scabs. Who would call us so early? We knew who.

Granny never said hello back, but she was there. She had called us every morning that past week, before the alarm went off and Mom had to wake up to open Sun-flower. Granny urged us every time to run away from home. "That man you live with is a wolf," she said again.

Our dad? She got the animal wrong. He was Moose, but we didn't tell Granny. We were taught not to talk back.

"You can't stay in a house," she said, "where you get hurt."

What did she mean? we asked each other by stretching our shoulders up to our ears. Then we tapped our temples to say, *How did she know?*

We hardly knew the route to school, around the block. We were only seven years old. Where could we go?

If our teacher had told us to run away, we would have. She was soft and warm and real. But Granny was a disembodied voice we never saw. Not even on video.

At first we lapped up every word she said. Mom's mom. How could a mom have a mom? That was almost like kids having kids.

"Tell me everything your folks do and say to you." Her voice was toothless and spongy.

We stared into each other's startled faces, looking for the right answer. All we saw was our reflection.

"I'm collecting evidence," Granny said. We wanted to ask what that word meant, but our lips wouldn't move.

The day before, Dad had said he would teach us how to drive, fast as a boy. He had slicked his hair back and flicked his cigarette ash on our shoes. "I'll make you a famous race car driver someday."

"Better to be safe," Mom had said, the shoulders of her T-shirt speckled with babies' spit-up, "and work at Lucky Seven."

If we shared that conversation with our Granny, would that give her evidence? And if she knew we wanted to be *faster* than a boy? Than a man? Than an animal? Would she say we were evil, too?

"They won't let you see me. Isn't that reason enough?" Granny asked.

We shook the phone to silently say, *That depends on whether Granny is good.* If she were in a movie, we would know. She would have cheeks like lollipops and would break into song. Maybe she had hamster cheeks or none at all. How could we tell?

We cupped our hands around the phone, pressed it closer to our ears. We might have heard our parents in their bed, turning in their dreams.

Once, we heard Dad call Granny a loon. We didn't know that was a bird; we thought it was a balloon, without the ball. Without the air that made it rise and fly and flee. The helium that had seeped into Granny's brain and made her float. Dad also called her airhead.

"Whose side are you on?" Granny asked.

Our side, of course. But whose side was that?

We didn't say yes, we would go. We didn't say no. We didn't say anything to Granny after hello except good-bye.

At breakfast, we asked Mom why we never saw *her* mom. Dad answered for her. "She doesn't live in our world. She sees things that aren't real." But so did we. We had imaginary friends. Then he asked, "You know what paranoid means?" We didn't. "What about schizo?"

We interlocked our fingers, tips touching each other's knuckles. Our free hands shoveled cornflakes into our mouths.

"Shoo now!" Dad said, with his mouth. With his hand he told us to hurry, to go get dressed for school. The swat was sweet, we tried to convince each other by squeezing the hams of our palms till the pain in our fingers was all we could feel.

We plucked our free hands from our pockets and scratched each other, catlike, on the arms.

"Why'd you do that?" Mom asked, and we couldn't tell if she was talking to just us kids or also to Dad.

We turned our lips inside out. Mom kissed our scratches.

"Don't coddle them," he said to her. Then to us: "Go, git."

Dad touched Mom's bottom while we craned around a corner, hiding. She didn't cry. She buried her hand down the back of his pants, and her face went all soft and mushy, like something was washing it away. It made our stomachs turn when she gave in to him.

After school, we invented games of tag. Runaway train, runaway horse, runaway cookie. "Run, run, cows to the slaughter. You can't catch me, I'm the gingerbread daughter," we chanted as the neighbor kids dragged us on the grass to pretend to bite our heads off.

Where could we run? Where would we stay? we asked each other. Up in a tree, hours away from the city, holding our breath, becoming the wind. In the triangle the seesaw made at the playground at school. Under the table in the teacher's lounge, the smell of coffee thickening our hides. In the supermarket bathroom, filching cold cuts and pound cake. In the back of the truck, like a dog on long road trips. He didn't suffocate. He could dig under the fence, but we had thumbs, so all we had to do was open the gate.

Dad gave Mom grocery money every week. If she weighed too much, he gave her less. One Sunday night we heard the creak of springs, her stepping on the scale, the needle wobbling as she shifted hips. We hoped she had peed before she stepped on it. A heavy bursting bladder could cost us how much cash for dinner? Could mean dry peanut butter sandwiches for lunch.

That week, her normal whisper broke. We heard her yelling from the bathroom scale: "Who made you boss of me?"

"You said you'd honor and obey," Dad said.

"What'd you expect? I was sixteen going on twelve."

"I rescued you from the garbage heap."

We knew it by heart, the origin story Dad liked to tell about Mom. How when they met, her dad was long gone, her mom was a loon, and Dad made Mom a queen. A goddess, even, in some versions. "You're nothing," was all he said this time, "without me."

We might have changed our minds and packed our bags, if Mom could come. Maybe she would.

We grabbed old lace curtains Ya-Ya gave Mom for arts and crafts. We tucked fabric into headbands for veils, into pants for trains. Two holey white tails trailed us. We pinked our cheeks and mouths with lipstick thinned with spit. Then we asked Mom to marry us.

A fuzzy bathrobe didn't cover her tiny purple night-gown. She pulled at her earlobes till we could almost see through them. Then she patted our bottoms. "I could eat you up."

"We'd never say, 'You promised to honor and obey.'" We mimicked Dad's bellow on the last word.

"Shh," she scrubbed the counter. Again and again.

"He's asleep." We slurped soggy flakes.

"Oh, he has spies." She laughed, but we couldn't see why.

Then our cereal spilled from the tremors of Dad's steps. "Hey, babe, how would you feel about . . . ?"

"I'd love to," she purred.

We couldn't hear what he asked into her ear, but we knew she always said yes. To *him*.

"What's with the getup?" Dad wiped sweat from the white T-shirt bunching on his chest, his plaid boxer shorts drooping.

"They want to get married," Mom said.

Dad kissed Mom in the ear, whispering her goddess name, Hera. He scratched Rex under the chin, then did exactly the same thing to Mom. She looked into his eyes, begging for more.

"I'll do the honors." He squeezed our hands together and smiled wide.

We couldn't tell him we wanted to marry Mom, then run away. We couldn't tell him we wanted to pull him up by his hair and make bald spots behind his ears. We couldn't tell him anything. He was the one, not Mom, who might really eat us up. We could almost see the fangs through his big grin.

The dark hair on his fingers felt like fur. His claws clamped down on our little knuckles. "Till death do you part," he said.

Whose death, of course, he didn't say.

6

Sometimes we scratched our husbands under the chin, but at that moment we vowed never to do it again. Never to do what he had done to her, even if she liked it.

Dad had worshipped Mom. That's why she stayed with him.

No.

Yes.

What did we know?

That she had stayed even after Shoes Day. That's what we called it, as if it came every week, between Tuesday and Wednesday, though it happened only once—as far as we knew.

Which was how far?

We answered the question at the same time by making a *C* with our left hands, marking the distance as the small space between thumb and index finger. *This much.*

The size of those leopard-print stiletto heels. The ones that girl-woman let us wear when we were only eight.

Pixie. Was that her real name?

7

Ya-Ya, our good grandma, always bought us shoes. Before our back-to-school shopping trip to prepare for third grade, she shoved a brush through our tangles till we cried. We bowed our heads as she sliced our scalp down the middle with the comb.

She made tight braids, "for no lice." Her own black hair, blooming gray, lay tightly wound on the back of her head. She wore a net she forgot to remove at the end of her shift, still reeking of grease and crinkle-cut fries.

She drove us to Penney's and parked between Patsy's Pet Salon and Sloan's Payday Loans. We didn't want to buy squeaky shoes that pinched our toes. Our soiled red Keds were comfy, but they didn't come clean, even after Ya-Ya rubbed wet fingers on them. "Spit shine your shoes, and nobody spit on you," she said. And then, "Shoes clean, no one look at holes in socks." Dad said everyone talked that way in the Old Country.

We plopped into the shoe department chairs and played with the measurement tools. "Where Marge?" Ya-Ya asked the only person in earshot.

"She retired," said a woman barely old enough to be called a woman. "I'm the new girl." Her name tag read, "Hi, I'm Pixie!"

"No, no. She not tell me. I go find her," Ya-Ya said to the Woman-Girl. Then to us: "You stay."

"She always leave you by yourselves?" Pixie asked.

We nodded.

"You could get kidnapped, you know."

We hoped she would kidnap us herself. We always wanted a big sister.

Pixie let us play dress-up. We wore peasant skirts and lots of pink, perfect for tottering in satin wedding pumps, in wedges and booties and espadrilles. In buckles and slip-ons. We were rock stars and mountain women. Goddesses in leather sandals strapped up our shins.

Our favorites were the leopard-print stilettos. Their heels bore holes in the carpet. They could gouge out eyes. We wrestled over who could wear this pair.

We pranced around, mimicking the sway of Pixie's hips, swishing our hair and pulling down our shirts the way she did. We wanted to see her breasts, so much bigger than Mom's. We wanted to grow them ourselves. Mom drank only coffee for breakfast and lunch so she wouldn't get fat. Maybe breasts were bad. Maybe we were, for wanting them.

"If your shoes are clean, no one will ask about your conscience." Pixie laughed at the way we parroted Ya-Ya.

We knew what a conscience was. We had seen *Pinocchio.*
A conscience was a little green bug.

When we tripped, Pixie helped us up and scanned us
for damage. "You Moose's kids?"

"Uh huh." We weren't surprised she knew Dad. He
was famous.

Her dress stretched and rippled with her belly laugh.
She lifted the soft curls around her ears. "He gave me
these. Real diamond studs. A hundred percent genuine."

We didn't ask why. He was Santa Claus to the world.

When Ya-Ya finally returned, she pinched our ears for
making a mess and a racket and being a nuisance. She
packed the heels back into their boxes and slammed down
the lids. "Marge not retired," she told Pixie. "Laid off. So
why they hire *you*?"

Why not? Pixie was the queen of fairies wearing sparkly
jewels. Couldn't Ya-Ya see that? "Look at her diamond
studs," we said. "They're from Dad."

Ya-Ya stopped stuffing paper back into the shoes we
had tried on. She stopped doing anything. She never held
still, except now.

We didn't buy shoes that day. Ya-Ya whisked us away.
We crammed our toes back into the too-tight tennies we
had outgrown in the space of a half hour. Stale grease and
crinkly fry smells trailed behind us.

"That Moose," Ya-Ya said, flooring the gas with her
lunch lady shoe. She mumbled in a mix of Greek and

English. "He want to kill me, too?" In an instant, we were back at Papu's funeral—Ya-Ya's face shrouded in black lace, our sinuses filling with snot.

She slammed the brakes in front of our house. On her rubber soles, she knifed her way to our door. Normally, we ran into our room to dodge the daycare babies, but today we wanted to hear what Ya-Ya would say.

She poured coffee and stretched her polyester pantleg under the Play Doh–covered table. We sat next to her, but she shooed us away. "Out."

We hid up in the leaves of the pear tree and watched Ya-Ya talk with her hands. We heard crying, even through the closed windows, but we often did. From babies or Mom, it was always hard to tell.

Ya-Ya slid a slice of cake across the table. The poppy-seed and honey one she baked us every week. Mom turned it into cubes, then dust. Pixie would have eaten it, and her breasts would have plumped into balloons.

We bit into pears so hard they hurt our teeth.

Ya-Ya waited till the daycare babies left, then helped us pack our clothes in black garbage bags. Mom taped a sign to the door on our way out: *Sunflower Closed Due to Illness.*

"What's wrong with you?" we asked Mom. Her eyes did look puffy.

"What's wrong with *me*?" She turned the car radio up louder.

At Ya-Ya's, we ate grape leaves and anise cookies. The grown-ups slept in the bedrooms, and we kids climbed under an electric blanket on the fold-out couch next to the kitchen. We dreamed we were flying.

And then we were. No, it was Dad, lifting us, still in our nightgowns, toting us out to the truck. Both at once, each in an arm. He lay us in the truck bed, covered us with a scratchy blanket.

The window to the cab was closed, but we still heard.

"Just this one night," Mom said. "And just because I don't want to wake up the kids again and make a scene."

"Please, babe," he begged. We could hear the mucus in his throat. We didn't like the sound of his voice dribbling down his beard in a puddle, the stop and go of his choppy breath. We didn't like it when he turned into the kind of rabbit Rex chased out of holes. We thought we knew how the world worked, but Dad-the-rabbit was from some other planet.

We pressed our hands against our ears, but the whole truck shook with his sloppy kisses on her knuckles, his little-boy babbling. "I can't live without you. I'll do anything to keep you. I'd drop to my knees if that wouldn't make me crash the truck."

We felt her breathe it all in. She laughed, a soft and satisfied sound.

"I wrote a song for you," he said. He sang about seeing her the first time. Their first date, first kiss, first dance. He sang about the day we were born. Even we would have given him whatever he wanted.

Then he fished a velvet box from his pocket and handed it to Mom. "Real diamond studs. They're yours now."

Had he pulled them right off Pixie's ears? We weren't about to ask. This whole fight was our fault for not keeping our big mouths shut.

"We'll stay," Mom said. "If you teach me how to drive."

"You already drive me crazy." The last word a playful howl.

"When I do this?" she asked, her voice a soft coo.

"Don't stop." We looked away though we knew Mom was rubbing his thigh or leading his hand to her knee. It's what they did at moments like this. It's how they made up, their words mushing into moans. We closed our eyes, in case we crashed.

We pretended not to hear, the anise cookies churning in our stomachs. The truck finally snugged in the driveway, and Mom and Dad rushed us to our room, eager to sequester themselves in their own. We faked sleep, but after they left, we tried to pierce our ears with our fingernails. We wanted to feel the way Pixie did. We longed for the sharp prick. We bit on a blanket to keep quiet once our skin started to bleed. Sunflower was closed at night. So if we cried, the babies couldn't cover up our noise.

Days later, Dad floored the gas, no slowing for curves. Next to him, Mom's breath came short and hoarse.

From the back, we inhaled her exhales, then squealed, "Rollercoaster!" This was Dad's cue to whoosh us down the hill as we lifted our hands above our heads.

"Whee!" To cover Mom's heavy breathing, we shrieked even louder this time.

"Stop!" Mom must have known he would slap her thigh when she said that. We knew to never tell Dad what to do.

"Ow," she said, but her lips curled up. We heard "meow," a purr.

Dad pimped the Bull with monster tires and ornaments. On Saturdays he drove us to the grocery store and smoked Marlboro Reds and listened to the radio while Mom dragged us through the aisles.

Sometimes we took too long. He drained the battery, and Johnny Cash ran out. He nodded off, the ashtray full, his chin, bearded in a week-old fuzz, falling into the fire.

That's how we found him, embers in his fur, when we returned. "The line was practically to Canada," Mom said.

"Time I teach you to drive." He had promised he would, the day we moved back from Ya-Ya's.

Mom and Dad switched seats. He showed her how to start the engine and steer. But she stopped too late and jerked the brake. "Don't give me whiplash," he said.

"Mmm," she said. A grunt that meant "OK."

He poked her in the ribs with his elbow. Her face now hot and pink, just like her clingy V-neck tee. Underneath we wondered if he had left a splotch of black and blue, green and purple. We would check next time we peeked into her bath. She always left the door ajar. A crack.

She said, "Mmm," again, but this time in a deeper voice, like a growling stomach.

When she swerved too sharp, he said, "Don't make me puke."

We leaned as far from the front seat as we could, dug our shoulder blades into the metal tailgate. We clenched our bellies and whispered to each other, "We could stop growing if we didn't eat so much. And the less we eat, the less Mom needs to drive to shop for food. The less she needs these lessons."

Every little failure brought his elbow to her ribs again. "Easy, babe," Dad said. "Why do you have to be such a woman driver?" The last two words like cussing.

"We'll grow our food," we said, hooking our pinkies. "We won't need to drive." We scratched together grubby scabbed-up elbows, girl to girl, to validate the vow.

"We can walk to school. And to work when we grow

up," we said. Dad couldn't hear us, though, over the cracking of his knuckles.

"Walk on the highway?"

"That's what the shoulder's for." We punched each other on the forearms.

"You hit like a girl," we said.

Then: "At least I don't drive like a woman." We hung our heads like cows.

"Will they let us walk if we work at Ford? They'll think we hate their cars."

"We do. We'll be crossing guards at school instead."

"Only if you share my corner."

"I'll be right across the street."

"Stop!" Did we say that? We thought we only wished that Mom would hit the brakes, that Dad would hit nothing at all. No one. But mostly not her, not her again. Please. We knew better than to breathe our thoughts out loud.

Then the truck came to a halt. We must have stopped it with our minds. We almost forgot we had that power. The kind we had wielded with The Groundhog.

"Get out." Dad snapped at Mom.

Dad switched seats with Mom and peeled onto the highway. "See how smooth I merged."

"Like a smooth shave." Mom's hand sandpapered against his chin, then grazed his lip.

He bit her finger and fondled the beauty mark above her lip. "I thought girls liked it rough."

"Mmm, good."

Who said that? We stopped our ears. We didn't want to know whose voice it was, his saying she had tasty blood, or hers telling him she enjoyed the hurt.

We looked only at each other so we couldn't see if he was driving with his hands or knees or furry chin.

Or with nothing—really? nothing?—but his mind. If we could make a truck stop with ours, we knew he could make one go with his.

Later, when Mom tucked us into bed, we asked, "Why do you have to learn how to drive?"

Her shoulders sank. Her ribs caved in.

"We can give up Brownies and birthday parties. Or we can walk."

She kissed our heads, lipstick pinking our parts. "Sometimes you have to be able get away. As fast as you can."

Where would she go? Dad would always find us at Ya-Ya's. Could we go to Granny's? Maybe we could fit inside the phone and find her. She might like Mom better if she could make herself that small.

"Go to sleep."

We burrowed under the covers and did what she said. We would be good so she would take us with her when she made her speedy getaway. We wouldn't even play with her phone anymore. Not much.

Mom killed the light, her skin flashing violet in the dark.

Dad left on another hunting trip. Instead of a rabbit, pheasant, or deer, he brought back lilies for Mom, the color of her tattoo. Last time, a slinky nightie. For us, licorice whips today. The time before, a bag of Swedish Fish.

"I'm sorry." He smoothed the errant hair behind Mom's ears, then kissed the top of her head. He said it again, falling to his knees and blubbering. "Remember when I took you to prom? You wore your hair like this. Remember our first Christmas? I gave you that V-neck." Remember this, remember that? He was always asking her to remember.

We wanted to forget how Mom rubbed against him so hard the whole room crackled with static.

We wanted to know if he ate what he shot, right there in the woods, sharing the meal with our dog, which was why he never brought it back. "Did he?" we asked Rex, his head on one lap, his legs on the other, as we swung on the bench swing in the backyard, gazing up at the stars.

Dogs never lie. If they're scared, they shake. If they're happy, they wag and lick. If they're sad, they whine. We opened Rex's mouth, searching for feathers or fur. But all we could see were black gums. If we were dogs ourselves, we could have pressed our noses to his tongue and smelled all the secret dark places he and Dad had been.

8

"If we were dogs we could have run away," one of us said.
The words, interrupting the movie in our heads, sounded like hail pinging off our boots.

"Isn't that what we did?"

"He treated Rex better than he treated us."

"He didn't teach him how to spell."

"Like that makes up for everything?"

"He gave us our first shot at celebrity."

"And our first . . ."

"What?"

But we knew. This back and forth. This yes and no. This you and me.

Our first glance at separation.

We had almost let it happen in the spelling bee. It was starting to happen now, our words knifing the air between us, even as we edged our bodies closer together for warmth.

We had made it stop before.

If we could just remind ourselves how.

9

*M*s. Rosen, our fourth-grade teacher, flitted by our desks, her breath in our hair. "Make a list. What are your parents good at? What could they share? I want them to join our classroom family." The last word, from her honey mouth, spellbound us. Could we have two families, one at home and one at school? One to run away to when the other became too much?

She swished her hair behind her shoulders, jingling her charm bracelet, fluttering the butterfly tattoo on her arm. Her skirt swirled against bare light brown legs. All our other teachers covered themselves.

We sisters made a single list, one girl writing what the other had whispered in her ear: Mom could do mom things. She could take care of us. So could every mom of every kid in our class. She had a beauty mark in the shape of a perfectly round jewel. But that wasn't a skill. We wanted our list to stand out, so Ms. Rosen would pluck it from the pile and smile at us and read it in front of the class.

We wrote:

Our dad's handwriting is so beautiful it should be in a handwriting museum.

He's so strong he can carry both of us at the same time.
He carries a map in his brain of the whole wide world.
He can spell every word in the dictionary.

We didn't tell her the other Dad stuff. The bad stuff he only did to us. No way we would tell. She had never read a list like that to the whole class.

"Pass your papers up," Ms. Rosen said, and we did.

We thought Ms. Rosen had never even read our pages. But later that year she asked Dad to help our class train for the school spelling bee. He was working the afternoon shift, so he could spare an hour after lunch.

The day he first visited our class, we were doodling in our notebooks—hearts and flowers and butterfly tattoos—while our teacher tried to explain the features of each Great Lake that made it great. Most kids peered at the beckoning world outside the window, the smell of dogwood wafting in. Some boys stared at their fancy yellow soccer socks. Some girls twisted or sucked or braided their hair. As soon as Dad entered the room, though, all eyes were trained on him at the front of the room.

He didn't look like any of the teachers, not just because he wore his factory clothes to school: blue jeans, tan boots, canvas button-up with the company logo sewn on. At home we got used to his bulging arms and towering shoulders. Here, he seemed to shake the industrial tile floors and the bumpy concrete walls with every step. When he talked, his voice drummed its own beat. "See?" we said to Ms. Rosen with only our eyes. "We told you he was special."

"You know what you win?" Dad asked the class. "Free plane ride, free food. Prize money. Forget the lottery, these odds are better. And you get to be on TV."

Now we all stretched our necks to hear. No one we knew had ever traveled on a plane. Most had never left Michigan.

Ms. Rosen held still in the chair behind her desk. Even her charms hung silent.

"You can't win by memorizing words," Dad said. "Not big, anyway. You have to learn patterns and rules. A little Greek and Latin. French and German."

Did anybody else's dad know foreign languages? He was smarter, even, than our teacher. He stored hundreds of years of knowledge in his head. Thousands. He knew about what had happened before the dinosaurs, even before Earth was formed in the solar system. And not because he had read so many books. Because he had been *there*.

No one would have believed us, so we didn't tell them. They might have taken us away, put us in a home where nothing ever happened. Where every weekend was as boring as a school assembly on bullying.

He taught us prefixes and suffixes. Rules and jingles. "*I* before *E* except after *C*." He taught us exceptions. "Every rule has an outlaw."

The outlaw words he set to hip-hop beats. He let us stomp our feet. He taught us how to close our eyes and wait for the words to arrive behind our lids.

On the day of the bee, Mom let us drink coffee for the first time, in a United Auto Workers mug. "Helps concentration," she said. Dad woke up early to see us compete. He made us eat toast sloppy with butter, even though our stomachs churned.

Mom stayed home. She could have asked Ya-Ya to watch the daycare babies while she was gone. That's what she did when she was sick. Instead, she said, "If I came, it would be bad for your nerves." Or hers.

We shuffled into the gym, in dresses that tied in the back, our feet pinched in polished patent leather. The spellers sat on the stage, the audience in folding metal chairs under basketball nets. At nine o'clock, Ms. Rosen started with the easy fourth-grade words Dad had drilled into us.

Then came the fifth-grade words and a tsunami of mistakes. First *bough. Exorcise. Crypt.* Finally, only we two stood. We could tell from Dad's wide eyes in the front row that he was already cashing our prize money check, eating our free food, flying on our free plane, watching us on TV, in his head.

"Despicable," Ms. Rosen said. We both spelled it wrong. Each time one of us failed, the other had to spell the same word right to win.

Words formed behind our eyes. "Imagine what winning looks like," Dad had told the class. We didn't like what we saw.

"Ten more minutes," Ms. Rosen said. "If no one wins after the buzzer rings, no one can continue to the next level."

"Weird" was the next word. An exception to the "*I* before *E*" rule. Dad had drilled that word into us so many times, not just at school but at home, we were full of its holes.

The rest of our class squirmed in their seats, their squeaks telling us *anyone* could spell that word. We closed our eyes and could see ourselves flying on the plane to the regionals. Smiling for the TV cameras. Dad hugging us the way Mom hugged the daycare babies.

We opened our eyes and saw his mouth gaping, ready to accept all the prizes the world was about to offer us. We smelled success on his breath, all the way from his first-row seat to the place where we stood on stage. It smelled like chocolate cake with whipped cream. But then we looked at each other and bit our lower lips in sync. *We* couldn't win. Only one of us could. We closed our eyes again and saw that plane, that stage, with only one of us there. We were so cold then, we had to grab each other's hands.

We wanted to win so bad, to make Dad proud. We wanted to earn the title Moose Jr. Finally.

We reached for it. We could taste the letters. The ones we wanted most. M-O-O-S-E-J-R. Cookie dough ice cream/candy kisses/guacamole and chips/extra cheese pizza, all rolled into one, the taste of winning. We closed our mouths and swallowed. We shut our eyes and imagined what we would see out the window of the plane, on our way, as winners, to New York City. The minutes stretched on almost as far as the miles separating us here from there.

We closed our eyes again. But now we looked harder. Only one of us, in this daydream, was allowed on the plane. The other stayed on the ground. And both of us were gasping for breath, about to pass out, the air so thin, our blood and guts and pee and sweat leaking out the part of us that was ripped. Broken in half.

"W-I-E-R-D," one of us said.

Wrong.

Now only one of us was left. One correct word and she was the winner. "W-E-E-R-D."

Air filled our lungs again. The pee ran down our legs only in our heads.

Dad shot up. "Give them another chance. They know that fucking word."

"Language, sir," the principal said.

"They. Know. That. Word." Rain pelted the windows, begging to be heard. "They know that word like they know their own names."

"Sir, I'm going to have to ask you to leave." The vice principal, bigger and badder than his boss, strode up to the front row.

"The clock is running," Ms. Rosen said.

The VP grabbed Dad's arm and tried to move him to the aisle, but Dad snapped free. Teachers corralled their charges, and parents scattered. The shouting and fleeing camouflaged the sound of the buzzer.

We squeezed hands. Maybe we had spelled the words wrong because of our shared DNA. Maybe we couldn't help but make the same mistakes. That's the story we told over dinner.

Mom made our favorite meal: roast chicken, mashed potatoes, and boats and boats of gravy. Her face had softened since the morning, perhaps from relief that the suspense was over. Maybe in sympathy that now we were like her. Unexceptional.

Dad grabbed two drumsticks from the chicken platter and banged them on his plate. "In boxing, they call it throwing a fight. It's against the rules."

We linked pinkies under the table. Blood pulsed through our hands, and we clenched our shoulders, turning our bodies to boards, waiting for the sound of his belt sliding out of his pants. Whenever we prepared, it didn't come.

Before we could lift a fork, Dad plowed through the food on his plate and ours. We shot a look at Mom, a plea for help, but she sidled closer to Dad. We could almost see the heat from his fingers, fueled by all the calories. He locked us in our room, through dinner, through breakfast and lunch the next day. Long enough to make us "remember this hunger."

For years he reminded us how smart we would have looked on TV. How tasty the buffet might have been. How good it would have felt to fly.

10

*M*aybe he was finally flying now. Up in the clouds, if we believed what Mom had said at the funeral, that he was the one making it snow. Maybe he had finally gotten what he wanted. Maybe, we said (more with breathy frost than words), we were off the hook.

Yes. Or no. Our bodies spoke for themselves. A nod so deep it was almost a bow brought blood rushing back to cheeks. A head shake—so wide it looked like a dog drying off from a bath—made earflaps slap against one of our chins.

Maybe we couldn't decide till we let ourselves grow up a little more.

11

The day we turned double digits, Mom finally gave in and let us stack our twin beds. We promised to take turns sleeping on the top bunk, which was of course the best.

Then Dad packed us in the Bull to drive to our present. He promised this would be the most kick-ass birthday ever.

This year we would get a pet. Rex didn't count. He wasn't ours. Everyone knew he was Dad's.

We wanted a hamster or a gerbil or a mouse or a hedgehog or a cat. Anything Dad couldn't take on a hunting trip. We knew the time was now. Not just because we had begged and begged. We had snooped.

Dad had been away on one of his many hunting trips. We found a bag, stuffed in the back of the master bedroom. No animal hid there. A living thing would suffocate in plastic, but we saw the animal's house. Too fancy to call a cage, it was more like a pet hotel or an amusement park, with bright yellow and red plastic tubes and a wheel with balls and bells. We wished we were small enough to live in it ourselves. We spent the rest of that weekend up in the pear tree considering names. Hairy the Hamster? Rapunzel the Rat?

On that drive, though, we couldn't tell Mom or Dad we knew what our present would be. We shouldn't have rifled through their closet, they would say. *Privacy* was one of Dad's favorite words.

So instead, we pinched each other's cheeks, opened our eyes wide, and asked, only with our faces, "Do we look surprised enough?"

Mom was nuzzled in next to Dad, shotgun. We sat in lawn chairs in the covered truck bed, holding each other upright as each curve in the road tried to dump us. The frayed plastic strips on the seats scratched the undersides of our thighs, below the short shorts Dad hated to see us wear. Mildew and motor oil smells mixed with Fuzzy Slippers, the baby-blue perfume Ya-Ya had given us as an early present.

We exited the highway, leaving behind the smokestacks and orange chemical burn from the few auto factories still standing. Asphalt turned to dirt. Rocky paths led to off-road riding. Dad loved to prove how much he needed his 4 × 4, even though he lived and worked in the city.

We stopped at what seemed like a random spot. No gate, no sign, no entrance to anything. We had never heard of state parks. Hiking? We just walked in the woods. Maps and marked paths were for sissies.

Dad blazed his own trail, and we followed single file, landing in the underbrush he had tamped down with tan leather work boots. We trampled ragweed, Queen Anne's lace. Ferns, pokeweed, and trees of heaven. Chipmunks skittered, pinky-size lizards scattered at the crunch of our sneakers, centipedes rolled into balls to play dead. Our noses tingled with pine and fresh sap.

It didn't matter that we couldn't see the way. Dad could, in his mind's eye. As we had told Ms. Rosen, our fourth-grade teacher, he had a map of the whole wide world in his head.

The June sky shone so clear and blue, we glimpsed the leftover full moon from the night before. We had no doubt Dad could navigate the heavens, too.

A shot dispersed a flock of geese we hadn't seen. Dad stopped, and we dominoed into his shoulder blades. "It's not hunting season," he said. "Some asshole must've gone and shot a squirrel." Dad pulled four flimsy orange vests from his pack and passed them down. "Not that you look nothing like critters," he said, "but any jackass fool enough to eat a furry rat might not be looking all too close." We slipped the vests over our heads and pretended they were bulletproof.

We knew enough not to ask "Are we there yet?" or "Where is that present you promised?" By the time Dad halted at a hollow log and patted the spots where we would sit, we were almost too tired to remember why we had come. The terrain splayed flat, Midwestern-style, wiping us out not with climbing but monotony.

He pulled a rifle from its case. We were used to that. But then he held it up to us and said, "I hope you like your present."

Mom kneaded her earlobes and jiggled her toes. She fingered her famous beauty mark, which was less than useless. Did she ever have any idea?

We wanted to chase a chipmunk and keep it in our pockets. We wanted to climb a tree and never come down. We wanted to be able to do real magic, so we could make Dad get us what we wanted, for once.

"But . . ." We couldn't admit we had seen the Hamster Hotel. Maybe he would give it to us at home? One thing for sure: we had no trouble looking surprised.

"I was ten when I got my first gun," Dad said. "Time you learned to use one."

We ferreted our fingers deep in the pockets of our cutoffs.

"Take it. You think it's going to bite?"

Dad might. He tossed the rifle our way, but instead of catching it, we ducked out of its range.

"What am I raising, pussies? It's not like it's loaded," he said.

We stood, keeping each other upright, as we had in the truck bed, this time not with our hands but our gaze. "We don't believe in guns," we said.

He elbowed Mom, and she offered a dutiful closed-mouth smile. "Guns aren't like God, for Chrissake. You don't have a choice to believe in them or not."

"What they mean," Mom stammered, but she didn't know, any more than Dad did.

"Guns kill people," we said.

"You don't think there was killing before?"

"It wasn't as easy."

"You know how simple it is to off someone with your bare hands? First thing I learned in the army. If I put my thumb right here . . ." He demonstrated on Mom's throat.

"Don't!" We wanted to knock him over; we wanted to cover our eyes. In the end, we did nothing.

He dropped his hands. Mom slumped down on soft moss and started counting under her breath.

He had almost killed Mom with his bare hands. We knew he could kill. And would again.

"You are way too easy to scare," he said. "Can't have that, once you're old enough to wield a weapon."

"We're . . ." What was the word? It started with a *P*. Something like pacifier.

"You're sorry?" Dad chuckled.

"We're pacifists."

"Ms. Rosen taught you that word?"

We looked down at our scabbed knees. Our teacher's name fell out of his mouth like a toad.

"Where does she think meat comes from? And I don't mean Burger King."

She was vegetarian, but we didn't tell Dad. We didn't want him to make fun of our favorite teacher. He leaned against a tree, and we could have sworn it swayed from his weight.

He tossed Mom a bag from his pack: bologna sandwiches, ridged potato chips, and Red Pop. "You start your lunch while I go take a piss."

At first we didn't wonder why he took our gun with him. In case he accidentally peed on a bear and had to defend himself? Had he said there were bears here?

The sun edged west from the middle of the sky by the time we realized he wasn't coming back. We didn't worry whether he was safe. He had the gun and cartridges. Nothing could hurt him anyway, not frost or fire. We had seen him weather all these ills without a hint of normal human pain. Even poison ivy left him alone. Ms. Rosen had taught us another useful word, as part of her fourth-grade mythology unit.

Immortal.

After a while, we had to pee, too. We didn't want whatever sucked in Dad to find us, so we barely left the trail.

Had he said we should follow? No cell service could reach such remote wilderness. Had we misheard? Had we listened at all? We stared at the trail ahead so long, squinting to catch a trace of his return, our eyes and brains went fuzzy.

"He must have told us to meet him back at the truck," Mom finally said, countless mosquito bites and goosebumps later. So much time had passed, our stomachs growled again, like our imaginary bears. Dad's trail had disappeared.

How could we find our way, without a map in our head? By the sun? Had we walked west or east? The full moon stared down, and we willed it to werewolf us so we could sniff our way home.

We had sprayed Fuzzy Slippers on our pulse points at breakfast. Every heartbeat magnified the perfume, and it spread across the whole forest, smoke signals saying, "Fresh young meat: come and eat."

Spiders and gnats haloed our heads. Chiggers and ticks were doing their invisible damage, we were convinced. Even our heads itched. Could we get lice from the woods? The centipedes no longer rolled over for us. They mocked us with their hundred legs. Even if we had had that many, we couldn't have caught up with Dad.

The air drained of pine and sap. Now it reeked of poison ivy and nettles. Salty sweat dripped into our throats, raw with an unfamiliar metal taste, perhaps a substance only known to double-digit kids. Ten might be kick-ass, sure, but who was doing the kicking?

"Which way do we go?" we asked Mom, but she didn't

know. Especially not when her nerves acted up. She breathed hard, and not from exercise. This always happened when we needed her most. As usual, she said, "Don't mind me. I'm just hyperventilating."

A shot rang out in the distance. Then a closer one. Maybe it was hunting season for twins.

We remembered Ms. Rosen's unit on current events. There had been a string of shootings all over the country, she had said. In movie theaters, elementary schools, and on college campuses. In churches and mosques. During marathons and in the middle of nothing at all. You could even watch reporters falling dead on TV.

The trees were alive. Or were we hearing squirrels moving through the leaves? Raccoons could be rabid, we knew. They had better not smell the dribbles from the Red Pop cans in our bags.

In the end, we found the right direction by choosing the opposite way Mom proposed. That usually worked. Or maybe we followed the shots. Even though we had learned the word *pacifist* in school, Dad knew what we *really* were. What he had made us.

Where does meat come from? Hunters. What do hunters use? Guns. We were so hungry by then we would have eaten a squirrel. A porcupine rustled above us, devouring the bark of a tree. Another hour out in the wild and we would have eaten him, too, quills and all.

When we looked away, the animal pounced and pushed us to the ground. Pee wet our downy legs.

But it wasn't a porcupine. It had soft fur like a bear. Like a beard. It was Dad.

He wasn't dead. Of course not. But—surprise!—neither were we.

"Was this some kind of trick?" we asked.

"Part of your present," he said. "I taught you how to navigate the woods. Only way to learn is to find yourself lost. That's how we did it in the army."

We stared at his throat, searching for the same life-or-death spot he had pointed out on Mom, wondering if our thumbs were large enough to press into it.

"And you followed the gun, instead of running away." He tossed us the rifle again. This time, we caught it.

We didn't dare ask what had happened to the Hamster Hotel. Next time we snooped in the master bedroom closet, all we saw were dirty shorts.

Instead, we did what usually worked to calm us down—pulled the guitar off its hook on the wall. We took turns playing with our naked thumbs. Our calluses grew with every strum.

12

After fall bled into winter, it snowed for a week. We plastic-wrapped windows and ski-masked our skin. "You look like a burglar," we said. Then: "I'm trying to steal a little heat."

"We're freezing our butts off," we told Dad, so he "reheated our backsides" with a slap of his huge hairy hand, the sting reminding us, every time we sat down, not to complain again.

One record-cold day, he shoveled the whole block. Neighbors parted drapes and watched from picture windows. He peeled off flannel, stripping to an undershirt tight enough to caress his pecs and showcase his thick neck.

Mom, in floor-length pink down, offered Dad coffee, but he waved her off. The steam might have melted him.

He built a snow fort and filled it with our sleeping bags and stuffed animals. Mom shouted from inside that we would freeze more than our butts, the whole night under the stars, but Dad wouldn't give in.

"It's too cold out there, even for the dog," Mom said.

"It'll thicken their skin. I slept outside in Alaska, and look what it did for me."

We didn't budge from the kitchen table. We didn't even shake our heads no. So he lifted us up, one in each arm, and carried us out to the fort.

We could hear him argue with Mom on the other side of the locked door. "You going to call the cops?" he asked. "You want those girls in foster care? I could even say the whole damn thing was your idea. Have you taken into custody."

We huddled on top of each other in the corner, the way the hamsters had in their cage in our second-grade classroom. We waited till the house went black, then sneaked off to Nevaeh's on the corner and hit her window with an iceball. Five throws later, she let us in through the basement door, her baggy narwhal T-shirt barely covering the letters on her days-of-the-week bikini briefs. We covered her mouth, the way Dad had so often covered ours. "Don't tell your parents we're here. We'll leave before they see."

We didn't tell her why we were there. We knew to keep our family secrets. We were special. We understood that Dad needed to train us the way he had been trained. Because we weren't human, exactly. A little bit less or a little bit more, we weren't sure. All we knew was that no one could know. "If you tell what happens in this house, you'll be taken away and never see your mom again," Dad told us long before we knew what the words "foster care" meant.

We slept on the floor, in the sleeping bags we had brought along, next to Nevaeh's bed. At dawn, we rose and fingered our way through her yard, down the block, back to our fort. Our house lay dark, the windows closed, the curtains drawn. We pretended to sleep. And waited.

Finally, Dad unzipped our sleeping bags. Mom clasped us to her chest, eyes bloodshot. She must have kept them open, staring at the ceiling, all night.

We ate bacon and pancakes, fuel for the fire in our bellies, Dad said. We inhaled all the air in the room, aiming to double our size and strength and pretend the cold night air had changed us.

Only when the phone rang did we notice we had lost our hats. Left them at our friend's. We knew the call came from Nevaeh's mom, from the way Dad's mouth curled into a fake smile.

"Nevaeh can bring the hats to school," he said. "They don't need them now."

He hung up, and his face twisted into a snarl. "So that's where you slept."

We held our guts to hold down our food. How could we have been so careless, unless we wanted him to know we couldn't handle the snow. Maybe we wanted him to see we could never be like him.

He plunged a hand into his front pocket and pulled out a pocketknife. We could feel our skin prick at the sight of it. What new rite would he perform with our blood? The worst part? We knew we deserved it.

"Give me your hands," he said. We could run but we couldn't hide, so we did what he said.

"It's yours." He laid the mother-of-pearl pocketknife from Alaska across both of our palms, the one we had coveted on Groundhog Day. His beard shook with silent laughter, enjoying, no doubt, our open-mouthed but silent shock. "You almost outsmarted me. I have to give you credit."

The knife burned from his body heat. It was a hot potato we passed between us.

"Keep it in your pocket. Next time you roam the streets at night, it might come in handy." He tousled our hair, his own callused hands softer than they had ever been.

Then he was gone.

When he returned from the basement, he lay two rabbit fur coats on our laps. He had promised to make them for us so long ago we barely remembered he had.

We wore the rabbit furs as if they were our skin. We wore them doing homework or watching TV. When it was too hot to wear them during the day, they blanketed our beds. Of course, the coats were the first things we packed in our bags, preparing for the sleepover party of our best friend.

Nevaeh was that rare thing, almost as good as a twin. She sat with us at lunch and gave us tropical fruit gum with a liquid heart and warned us when the teacher was looking so we could stop chewing. She lent us a swipe from her root beer lip gloss, and we swooned in a sticky girl clump, drunk from the fumes.

After school, we raked the lawn, building piles of leaves so big that bears could have lived in them. We scooped up decomposing mounds, their wet fermented smell pickling our fingers and sliming our pants.

That's when Dad told us why we couldn't go to Nevaeh's party. "You can't trust people outside of the family. You shouldn't tell them anything."

"But Nevaeh is almost like our sister. Mom will say yes. Mom always says yes."

"You talking back to me?"

"No. You're reading our minds."

"OK, smart-ass. No sleepovers. Ever. No eating at anyone's houses, either." Dad scooped a confetti of leaves and showered us with them, leaving a dirty trail on our freshly washed hair.

On the school bus, the Friday before the party, the girls who had been to sleepovers before said that in the dark all the secrets came out, the ones that bonded best friends. Without us there, on the other side of midnight, Nevaeh might become some other girl's best friend. No one would learn our secrets. Like the one about how Dad had killed his dad. Nevaeh's mom might have called the cops, and they might have dumped us in a foster home. No wonder we weren't allowed to have sleepovers.

In the cafeteria, the Monday after the party, Haley, our second-best friend, told us what Nevaeh had told her, after the parents snored and the house filled with spooky rattles and creaks, during that flash of in-between time after the night and before the day.

Nevaeh had said she only hung out with us at school because she had known us since kindergarten. That now she had grown out of us.

Then, later that day, as the bus bumped over potholes, Haley whispered to us that another girl had said we were stuck-up. And a few of them had called us skeletons, just like our mom.

We trudged home from the bus stop and stuffed our mouths with so much peanut butter and jelly we wanted to throw up. But we didn't. We needed to keep the sandwiches down so we would grow breasts like Nevaeh's, because we secretly suspected what she meant when she said she had grown out of us was that she wore a bra already, but we didn't yet need one.

The next morning, we squeaked the daycare babies' caterpillars and placed the tiny people around the dollhouse kitchen, pretending we were playing with them as a joke. We hated Mom for leaving the toys out to tempt us, and we hated ourselves for hating her.

We hated babies, too, though the baby in the dollhouse in its teeny tiny cradle was so adorable we had to slip it into our pockets and smuggle it to school.

At lunch, Nevaeh said that Haley had said, deep down in the dark, that she thought we couldn't do sleepovers because we wet the bed or sucked our thumbs. Or both.

On a field trip to Fantasyland, a display of Christmas decorations at the rec center, everyone talked about their crushes. They wouldn't name names, but everyone knew—everyone who went to sleepovers. They said they could only reveal the identities of the school's cutest boys in the part of the night when the sky glowed so black it glinted blue, like the hair of you-know-who. No, we didn't know.

"That's when the magic happens?" we asked. "Only after midnight?"

"It's not magic," Eliza said. "It's like being drunk. You know how grown-ups only tell the truth if they've been drinking?"

Dad fed us spoonfuls of whiskey when we had a sore throat, and the liquor burned like when we washed a cut, so that probably didn't count. "Your parents let you drink?" Were we missing that, too?

"Not that kind of drunk," Eliza said. "The kind where you stay up till you're so sleepy you're dizzy and kind of tipsy and you have to lie down or else you'll fall but you're too excited to go to bed, so you're like an asleep-awake zombie."

"I know," they all said.

When we came home from school, we emptied the toys from our closets and bins and donated them all to Mom's daycare babies. We decided that, every day from now on, we would bypass the bunnies and Barbies and lock ourselves in the bathroom in the morning. We would spend every minute before we had to catch the bus smoothing our hair and choosing our underwear.

One morning our messy buns kept falling out and tumbling over our eyes. Dad yelled, "You're going to be late." He always said that, but he was always wrong. Until we missed our bus. By a hair.

"Don't give them a ride," Dad commanded Mom. "They've got to suffer the natural consequences, or they won't learn."

We walked two miles to school. Rain pelted us the moment we stepped outside. We could have sworn Dad had gashed a hole in the cloud to punish us.

We learned a lesson, all right—that Dad was a prick. We gnawed the skin on our fingers, making them bleed, cutting ourselves up for using that word. It was a tough word, and we had to toughen up or no one would invite us to parties, even in the daytime, anymore.

We decided to get "drunk" at home. We stayed up

Friday night, after lying quietly in bed till we heard our parents' slow breath from behind their closed door.

We whispered, bunk to bunk, willing our eyes to open wide, listening to the strange sounds our mouths made— garbled, slurred, and sloppy. We didn't dare climb out of bed. We would have tripped all over ourselves.

We told each other our crushes, not just on boys but on teachers. On actors, singers, and athletes. Even on other girls. We were in a half-dream, half-awake state. We told each other we could fly. Weren't we doing it right now in our beds? Or were we only in our heads? The space between the two worlds shrank as small as the smallest hours of the night.

13

We were so quick to forget all he gave us—the pocket-knife, the rabbit furs. Not so fast to forget he was a prick. That word, the one we slung in middle school, shouldn't still be our favorite insult. Hands on hips, mouths puckered into pouts. Chins turned up to the sky, defiant.

We thought everything about our lives would be different now than it had been back then. We made plans. We wrote them all down, which was supposed to make them real.

14

We decided to write a letter to our future selves. We squeezed our knees together in our cramped closet, flattening the Game of Life with our elbows, pillowing our heads with the down coats we had let fall from their hangers. We uncapped a pen that leaked black ink onto our chipped fluorescent-blue nails. Black and blue was our favorite look. We even dyed the tips of our hair to match.

We wrote in a small notebook whose metal spirals were as raggedy as our fingers.

Dear Future Us:

We're in seventh grade.

We live in a little room with two bunk beds and one tall dresser and one desk and two chairs we have to move to the kitchen when it's time to eat dinner.

We never "fall out of bed." We never "bump into the furniture." That's just code. Don't forget what it *means*.

Don't forget, because people might say it to you. They might look at their shoes and swear they tripped on the stairs. And you'll know they're lying.

We like fuzzy socks. Fuzzy ski caps. Fuzzy sweaters.

We're five foot five and ninety-seven pounds, and we

can't get rid of the big red pimples on our foreheads, even when we scrub so much with witch hazel that our skin becomes thin enough that we can almost see through to our cheeks.

Maybe they're lying to protect someone, so don't call them liars. Just braid their hair and share your gum.

We spend most of our time staring into space. That's not true, but it's what Mom says.

Really, we're thinking. Things like:

Are we ugly or pretty, straight or gay or bi? Smart or nice? Do we have to choose? Do you have to be one thing and not another thing at the same time?

We don't know if we could ever love anyone as much as we love each other, and we're both girls. Does that make us queer? Does Nevaeh think we are? Do we love her? In *that* way? What about Bo?

Sometimes we want to be boys. Is that bad?

Sometimes all we want to do is take a shower and imagine that the first violin or the first viola is in the stall with us. The first violin is a boy, and the first viola is a girl. They both have long hair and perfect pitch.

We don't want to go to school. School is either too hot or too cold. It's too early and we're too tired. Lunch is late, so we're always hungry, and we're not allowed to eat in the orchestra room anymore because our teachers say the crumbs will attract rats.

School is an endless string of socially awkward encounters. "Pass me that pencil. Let's make small talk. Do I know you? Do you like me? I mean, Do you like-like me?" The other part of school, the part that isn't stressful, is boring. And then some parts are stressful *and* boring at the same time.

Do our teachers like us? Do all our friends talk behind our backs at the sleepovers we're not allowed to go to?

What do people say about us? Is it true? Have they figured out our codes? Do they know what we *mean*? Or do they just hear what we say?

We don't know if we're special or if we just think we are. We don't know if we're good or bad. Santa Claus knows. We wish we could still believe that. We don't know anything, to be honest. By the time we read this again, we'll be old. Then we'll know everything.

All we know now is this:

We'll always be together.

We sealed the letter in a box with the label "Open in ten years." By then we would be grown up. Not like our parents, though. We would still be kids inside. Always. We would never let our kid brain die, never forget what it felt like to be us right now.

We would have no more questions. That's what we really thought.

15

*B*ut now?

The wall of the church scratched our backs, even through thick coats. The brick didn't budge. Neither did we.

One of us said we should stop this nonsense already. What were we learning that we didn't know?

The other urged us on. We were almost there, weren't we? Almost to the part of our lives where we became who we were now.

The part that would explain why we did what we did to Dad.

The red-hot part of our lives. It started between our legs. It began with the guns locked behind a door. It hid itself in the underwear drawer. *That* part.

16

We both started our periods the same day. Mom pointed out her pads under the bathroom sink and said, "Help yourselves," which sounded like, "Don't ask me, I'm busy." We didn't need to. We had each other.

Dad was working the afternoon shift at Ford. Mom had closed Sunflower for the day and gone to the hospital. "Nerves," was Dad's only explanation. Perhaps he thought we would understand, now that we were thirteen. We didn't want to know if "nerves" would happen to us as we ripened and matured. If black eyes would appear in our sleep, as they did with Mom. If we would cower and lower our voices till all sound disappeared.

We craved rare steak. We wanted it so much we almost smelled it. The scent of our bodies.

We bit into apples and left our marks in front of the boys at school. But we were afraid of tampons. They could violate us. We were sure they would hurt. If they got stuck, how would we coax them out? Would we no longer be virgins?

No matter how much Mom cleaned, the cracked linoleum and stained carpets always reeked of warm milk and pureed peas, diaper rash and ear infections. Everything we had went to Mom's daycare babies. Our old toys lined the living room on rickety shelves: ponies with pink hair, hamsters on trikes with removable underwear, plastic squirt guns that glinted like metal.

The real gun belonged to us, whether we wanted it or not. Our birthday present, back when we had actually asked for a hamster.

That afternoon we opened the gun safe. Did Dad really think we didn't know where he had stashed the key? He hid it in his underwear drawer, which meant he wanted us to find it.

We were just going to look at it, we said. Hold it. Caress its octagonal barrel, long and strong. Take it apart. Smell the metal, unbreakable and cold. We just wanted to dry the inside, rub linseed oil on the warm brown wood of the stock with a soft white cloth. Cleaning a gun wasn't so different from cleaning a flute. Our orchestra teacher let us try out all the instruments. You have to keep your equipment pristine, he said, or it won't do what you ask it to.

The Winchester was an antique, Dad said, a present from his dad, which he had passed on to us. We would give it to our kids someday, we told each other, as if we would share our children the same way we shared everything else and we twins would live in the same house forever.

We fingered the action, breaking it open to wipe it down. We polished it. We stroked the trigger and trigger guard till they gleamed, the bolt and bolt handle, stock and forestock, sight and muzzle. We left the safety for last. Or maybe we forgot it. We were always forgetting things.

We made music, one of us playing guitar while the other played with the gun. One had better pitch, the other better aim.

Behind the curtains, we watched squirrels and cats, little kids on Big Wheels, teenagers in baggy pants leaning on telephone poles, their pockets bulging with baggies. We pushed the muzzle through the musty cloth, aiming out the corner of the window, telescoping up and down our block, taking turns. We were just looking, we said. No different from using binoculars. The magazine was empty.

At first we made sound effects to mimic pulling the trigger. But soon that wasn't enough. We wanted more. More power, more fire, more action. The more the gun gleamed, the more we wanted it to blind us.

We were the gun. We were one with it.

We found Dad's ammunition in his other drawer, under the condoms and lube. Next to a photo of a boy we didn't know. He reminded us of someone, but we couldn't remember who.

Our blood ran hot. It bubbled up to our fingertips. We don't remember which one of us aimed and which one watched.

We pointed at a squirrel. They were always stealing seed from the birds. "Vermin," Dad called them. "Pestilence." He said we should catch them in traps and feed them to dogs. If he were there with us, he would say, Stop thinking and do it.

We shot. The rifle bucked, and we fell back, onto the guitar and each other.

Only then did we see that the squirrel looked like the stuffed animals we had clutched to our chests not so long ago in bed. The discarded toys that stared at us from the plastic bin near the TV.

The turkey vultures would tear the animal to pieces before Dad returned from the factory. But not before we tore into ourselves. We scratched our arms till they turned red, bit our fingers bloody.

We should have buried the squirrel in our yard. Or dug a hole and thrown in the entire afternoon. We wanted to lock the gun away and hide the key better than Dad did. We wanted to bury it. We wanted to bury everything that just happened, then throw ourselves into the hole. But instead, we took turns prancing through the living room, past our old army men, our dolls and bears and blocks, our squeaky balls and crinkly chickens, past all we had toyed with and then, much too quickly, tossed aside.

In eighth grade we joined track and sprinted in spandex and sports bras. After practice, we strutted home with our sculpted abs bare, hair flying down our backs, over shoulders, into everybody's business.

See our hips? our clothes said. See the dip from our blossoming chests to the tiny slip of our waists?

"Cover up," Dad said, so we did. But only while he was looking. When he spotted us on a run, he yelled out the window of the Bull, "Cover your ass, if you don't want it grabbed."

Back at home, we gave him lip for harassing us. "For protecting you," he said.

He wouldn't grab us like that. But was it true, what he said, that every other man and boy wanted to? That we were taunting them?

"Play outside," he commanded, as if treating us like kids would stop our nipples from poking through our shirts.

When we didn't respond, he pushed us out the door. We thought every dad moved their kids that way—yanking arms. swatting butts, squeezing shoulders so tight they might never be able to shrug again.

Too old to play, we sat in the yard watching our dog hump the rug he had dragged out of his doghouse, then shaking him off when he targeted our legs.

We used to think Rex was hugging us. In fourth grade,

we had asked Mom, "Can people only get pregnant when they're in heat, like dogs?" In fifth: "How do babies get out of their mothers' belly buttons?" Our sixth grade "family life" curriculum taught us girls cures for morning sickness and stretch marks, what to expect from Caesareans and epidurals. No one mentioned how the baby wormed its way inside. What the boys were learning in a separate classroom was a mystery.

In seventh grade our gym teacher taught health once a month. She wore a whistle so loud it could have scared away bears. We set up folding chairs on one side of the basketball court and listened to her explain why she couldn't have a baby. Then she told us not to laugh at boys when they "got their little boners." The older people get, the more they will say anything, our silent open mouths said. The first thing they lose is their embarrassment.

We buried our heads in our armpits. "Boys can't help themselves," she said, echoing Dad, "when you dress like you do." She looked at us two, but we knew she meant all of us in the room. All the girls in the world.

Finally, in eighth grade, we had real sex ed. Ms. DeMeter, in cornrows and basketball shorts, passed out condoms and cucumbers. We choked back questions like "Do they ever get this big in real life?"

We didn't titter. We sat, serious and still, pretending not to want to sprint away from all this.

We were fecund and fertile. We were nubile and knew it. Mom's long-ago words echoed in our heads: "You're my too, too much."

After school, we climbed the pear tree and hid in its multiplying branches, waiting for dark. We slipped the school-issued condoms from our pockets and inflated them, smothered them in cherry lip gloss, and licked them like lollipops.

After sex ed, we claimed not to be virgins. "Only virgins sleep in pajamas," we said, wearing T-shirts to bed.

"Only virgins wear dresses," we said, hooking thumbs through our belt loops.

"Only virgins live in Virginia."

"That's why we're in Michigan. A place so cold it's shaped like a mitten."

"Or a boxing glove."

We pretended to be cold and callous, too. As tough as the statue of Joe Louis's fist Dad liked to drive by downtown. We rejected every boy in our grade who asked us out. We didn't need boys when we had each other. That was our story, anyway.

But Bo didn't like to be told no.

He lived on our block and watched us glide down the street in little more than underwear. "You're so hot," he said. "I got some ice-cold pop to cool you off."

Bo had known us since our mothers pushed us all

around in strollers. We would run through sprinklers with him in nothing but Pull-Ups. Sure, we had been sweet on him when we were younger. We had all played Red Light, Green Light. Freeze Tag. Statues. We had ridden our bikes together in the sticky weather and shared melting candy bars in the sun.

"Orange Crush?" we asked.

"With a straw?" He knew us too well.

We let him lead us on—up his step, onto his porch, into his room, where he opened us each a can of sticky froth.

We knew about him, too. How he lived with his mom, who worked at the same factory as Dad and wouldn't be home till six. It was only four.

Bo's house sagged. It was even more cramped than ours. His porch crumbled under our sneakers, and the holes in his screen door let in bugs as big as birds.

His room smelled like formaldehyde and chocolate milk. Science class and the school cafeteria. The sandbox at the playground where we used to bury his tow trucks and toes. The kiddie pool in his backyard, before it was turned into a flower pot. The plastic lion mask he let us wear for the kindergarten parade on Halloween. His walls were covered with football and hockey memorabilia from games at Pontiac Stadium and the Joe Louis Arena. If we could have bottled his room as a perfume, we would have called it Boy.

"We're friends, right?" he said. "I'll show you mine if you show me yours."

As little kids we had sat on the curb, waving to cars as they passed. Once a man stopped and rolled down the window. Bo had grabbed our hands and yelled, "Run!"

We had the same feeling at that moment that we had had then, half lured in, half pulling away. We sat in his room the way we sat in our bodies. Not knowing we had a choice.

"Take it all off," he said.

At first we just stared. He was too small to play football, too big to look like a nerd. He was cute in the way Mom's daycare babies were. But maybe we thought that because we had seen him in a diaper.

We sisters pressed our legs into each other's. We sat on the edge of Bo's unmade bed, but somehow our backs were against the wall. His jeans moved. We started to giggle, then pressed a hand over each other's mouths. *Don't laugh when those poor boys get their little boners.*

We could see in the way he hunched forward in the chair, his chin almost on his knees, what he was trying to tell us. That there are things they don't teach us in school. Things we need to know.

"Just for a look. Pinky promise," he said. *They can't help it when you dress like that.*

We were little kids again. We had played doctor at

eight, nine, and ten. But back then, we had nothing to show.

He started to strip, and so did we. We didn't expect him to wear boxers, like Dad. If only he had had briefs. His bare legs were as sweaty as his face. We stood on display, all three of us, cold and silent as skeletons in science class.

"You have hair," he said. "I've never seen so much."

Maybe we really were wolves. "We thought you never saw a girl before. That this was educational."

"There's this thing called the internet," he said. "Maybe you heard of it."

We pulled the bedspread over our shoulders and slumped back on the mattress.

He preened, his chest stretching across the room. "Don't tell me girls don't sneak it, too."

The Crush bubbled up from our bellies, through our throats, oranging our eyes and ears.

He pulled on Redwings sweatpants. "Do something for me."

"We have to finish our run." We zipped back into our body-hugging pants, our tiny clingy sports bras, and prepared to finish our three-mile warm-up.

"Not now. Tomorrow. Let me kiss you both in front of my locker, when everyone's looking."

"You said we're just friends."

"We can pretend. I want people to think I can handle two girls at once."

"We don't think so."

"Then I'll tell everyone you came to my house and showed off your cunts."

"But we didn't."

Or maybe we did. He would say so, and that was practically the same thing. All we could do was storm to the door and slam it behind us.

He followed us onto the porch, the concrete crumpling into his dirty socks. "Your word against mine. I can say whatever I want. Two at a time. Ménage à trois."

We crammed our feet into our shoes. "We'll tell everyone you dropped your pants for *us*."

"Please do. Know what they'll call me? Lucky. And you? The slutty twins."

We tied our laces so tight they hurt. Maybe he had heard us in the pear tree, pretending not to be virgins. Maybe saying or even thinking something makes it so. When we had wanted The Groundhog to see his shadow, he had seen it. When we had wished to be in every class together, we were. If Dad could climb McKinley without a rope, maybe we could make our thoughts materialize. Even if we weren't wolves, we might not be quite human, either.

"You know what they'll say," Bo shouted as we ran away. "Why did you wear skimpy clothes?"

We also heard what Bo didn't say, what we knew others would, if we blabbed: *Why did you ask for it?*

We stopped our run short, heading into our house. The skin on our strong bare bellies pleaded with us to cover it up, so we shielded our navels with our forearms, even before Dad opened the door. "I warned you," he said, reading our minds or our limbs. "Next time you go outside, wear some clothes."

We jumped in the shower and tried to disappear down the drain. We grabbed a towel, and it swallowed us. We had to push and shove and ferret our way out. We would have to find our bodies again, lost in oversized sweatshirts, even if it took a whole year.

17

*W*hoosh. Whatever wasn't covered shocked from the sharp wind. Nose, mouth, teeth. Nostrils, lashes, tips of ears. The liquid lubricating our eyes almost froze stiff.

That's what happens when you don't cover up, our bodies were telling our brains. Our thin skin said, *Dad was right; it's dangerous out here.* Here meaning everywhere.

He was just trying to keep his girls safe.

Like they do in Saudi Arabia.

18

In eighth grade, the graffiti on our lockers had read, "Instant orgy. Just add one." The janitor painted over it the next day, but our nickname stuck. "The Slutty Twins" followed us to high school.

At first we tried to slough the label off. Us? Sluts? Middle fingers in the air, arms up like the half-naked Statue of Liberty herself. *Give me your hungry. Give me your horny. Give me a break. Slut you!*

When that didn't work, we tried burying our breasts in sweatshirts that would practically cover the whole country. For a year we wore prim button-up collars. One-piece bathing suits. "Granny gowns." Even men in cars stopped catcalling. Guys didn't seem to see us at all.

But our music drowned under all that fabric. If we wanted to play, we had to unzip. So now, at fourteen, we changed our clothes and named our band the Slutty Twins.

"What's that mean?" Mom asked, when she saw us inking posters on the kitchen table for a gig in our friend Haley's garage.

"It's what they call us at school, so we co-opted the term."

"You what?" She readjusted the baby on her hip and leaned in to hear. We rolled our eyes. We knew she hated when we used fancy words. But at that age, we loved feeling smarter than she was. She didn't know the latest memes. Couldn't recognize our favorite YouTubers. Texted with one finger.

When we explained things we didn't think needed explaining, we talked too fast. At least that's what Mom always said. We didn't mean to. "It's like *queer*," we said. "Like *bitch* or *nerd*. If you use it on yourself, you take the venom out of it. You say: You can't hurt me with that word anymore. It's mine."

Maybe she heard us, maybe not. She was busy patting the whining homunculus on the back. Lifting him up and down, squat and rise, her baby-elevator trick that doubled as a workout.

Even without our kiss, Bo got his wish. He made the cut for the football team. Rumor had it he could take on the whole starting lineup for girls' field hockey, all at the same time. What we believed? That he could find a picture on a porn site and Photoshop their faces in.

When people at school asked what we meant by the name of our band, we would whip out our phones and play them a riff we had recorded. A guitar lick that could suck them dry.

Dad didn't like our "indecency," but he let us play anyway. "Only," he said, "because music was what you were born for." He had always told us we were better than anything on the radio. He had played guitar since before he was born. That was his story: *before*. He played all instruments, but cymbals best. He played with the seasons and the atmosphere. He played us to sleep and, too often, woke us up with dissonant chords after midnight. We had strummed along since we could remember.

We played in our bottom bunk, heads bumping the sagging springs above. We played in our unfinished basement, orange mold mountains and waterbugs our only audience. We played in our garage, cowering under power tools that spontaneously turned on from the vibrations of our amps. And inevitably, we posted our songs on the internet.

In the clips, we dressed almost alike, in jeans and sweaters. One loose, one tight. One virgin, one whore. The two twin states, mirror images, sullied and pure. Like the two of us, virtually identical.

We played for our fourteenth birthday party. We were technically a duo, not a band. Paula on lead guitar and vocals. Artis on bass and drums. In black bottoms, white tops, and Dominatrix boots, we looked like waiters in a fancy restaurant that cooked up the customers.

We crammed into our one-car garage. It crackled with the surplus Christmas lights Dad bought one year but couldn't afford to turn on, bulbs in every shape and color. Pelts and antlers swung from the ceiling, and weed whackers and power drills dangled too close to our heads. We belted out every beating to our butts and our brains. We sang out our family secrets in codes even we couldn't yet understand.

We played the soundtrack to the movements of our bodies, the movies in our brains, and our hormones and growing pains turned electric.

Dad joined in the performance, commandeered the drums, adding unbidden cymbals. It was hard to distinguish the instrument from him. It sounded like his boom when we forgot to wipe our feet. Like his bellow when he didn't approve of our clothes.

We danced in a trance while we played. Our friends couldn't help but copy. Nevaeh and Haley. Marietta and Eliza. Gigi and Nikki. Not Bo, but who needed boys?

With so little air, we stripped down to sports bras, forgetting Dad was there. We twirled and sang and strummed and banged.

No, we didn't bang, Dad did. Or was it thunder?

He picked up our shirts and snapped them at us.

Clang clang clang. Our eardrums popped. Lightning struck the driveway and ignited the asphalt. Everyone emptied into the street, away from the flame. Without all those bodies crammed together inside the garage, we shivered and pulled our shirts back on.

Then—and this is the weird part—it rained for one hot minute. Just enough to put the fire out.

We touched each other's sleeves to share what we knew in a flash: that the fire stopped *because* we had covered ourselves. Dad wasn't just playing with our band. He was taking command.

We kept strumming and singing. Thunder backed us up. Dad danced next to us, moving his arms to the weather's jaggedy rhythm, bumping his elbows into our ribs to remind us he was there.

"Do we need to go in?" we asked him, at the end of our song.

"No," he said. "I made it far away this time. But I can always make it close." His fingertips burned our cheeks. We smelled burnt hair, and our messy buns loosened, strands falling out over our faces.

He *made* the thunder and lightning? Was that the real reason we couldn't invite our friends to spend the night? Why he had banned us from sleepovers?

He buried his hands deep down in his pockets, and his face darkened to silence us.

After our final song, with real-live thunder keeping our beat right outside the window, our friends followed us into the kitchen. Ya-Ya waited with the same pineapple upside-down cake she baked every year. Mom, Dad, Ya-Ya, and all our friends tried to crowd around us at the Formica table. Some had to stand in the doorway.

We lit fourteen candles, and our friends sang, "Happy birthday, Slutty Twins. Happy birthday to you."

"What you call them?" Ya-Ya slid her glasses down her nose, caught a stray hair from her bun, and smoothed her best dress. Even in her special occasion clothes, she still smelled of stale grease and crinkle-cut fries.

"That's the name of their band," our friends said. "It's ironic."

"Like opposite?" Ya-Ya looked at Dad, who grew up as her translator.

"Like playing with fire," he said.

We blew out the candles, wishing Ya-Ya would make her cakes right-side up once in a while.

"In Old Country," Ya-Ya said, "we were virgins on our wedding night."

"They're not saying they're not virgins," Mom said. "They're just saying . . ." Did she know what we were saying?

Haley stepped in. "They want to change the meaning of *slut*."

"Like it can mean you have a passion for something," we said. "You can be a book slut, say, if you like to read."

"What about their hymen?" Ya-Ya asked.

Mom ignored our hymens and brought our presents to the table. We opened boxes of lip gloss and origami money cranes, envelopes weighted with gift cards. Ya-Ya gave us shoes. She always gave us shoes. Shiny, sturdy, respectable. Little kids' shoes. Virginal shoes. School girl shoes. Mary Janes. The kind of shoes it would be impossible to have sex in.

"Shoes shined, conscience clear."

Our friends looked to us to translate Ya-Ya, but we just rolled our eyes.

On the internet, our viewers clamored for more. So we uploaded new songs, with new outfits and dance routines. We wore "costumes," not our real clothes. We were characters, not ourselves. We painted our mouths cinnamon red-hot, parted our lips, and made a little pout. We set the filter to create a soft, hazy light. It was all ironic, though. Right?

When strangers told us online we were hot, when anonymous comments arrived asking us what we were wearing, what we slept in, the color of our underwear, we didn't bolt the way we did when men whistled on the street, catcalled us at the mall or library, licking us up with their eyes. The screen seemed to shield us.

We channeled every starlet, every diva, every heart-throb, every voice, every thrust of hip and dip of the chin.

Dad said we had inherited his musical genius. He told us we were divine. And, finally, we believed.

We could lure and sway. Better yet, we would finally be able to run away.

We would find a way to monetize the songs, to sell the data they collected or make listeners watch an ad. If we figured it out, we would be able to buy a house. For us two. For the times when Dad's thunder and lightning were not just part of our backup band. We knew what he could do. He had warned us. We could buy a house for Mom. *She was so small she could have squeezed between the bars of a cage.* But she wouldn't. Not unless we gave her someplace else to go.

At fourteen, we didn't know what "jailbait" meant. Strangers used that word in the comments they left after watching us perform our songs.

We didn't foresee that "slutty twins" would be one of the most common phrases in the history of internet searches. People weren't looking for us when they typed the phrase in. But when we popped up, they made us into everything they had been searching for. We didn't know we would go viral.

We couldn't keep up with the comments. We couldn't even count them. No one seemed to realize anymore that the name of our band was ironic.

We were followed on social media and on the street. By now we covered our bellies and our asses when we ran. We would have covered ourselves in a sheet like we did for Halloween in second grade if that would not have attracted even more attention. We were two, we were strong, we were fast. But what if next time we weren't fast enough?

One evening, on our after-dinner run, a man with a half-zipped fly and a fistful of daisies chased us, shouting, "Wait up, Slutty Twins." We sprinted ahead but not so far we didn't feel the flowers he threw hit our asses.

Inside, we changed into sweats, then told Dad. The ends of his mouth curled up toward his eyes. "What did you expect with a band name like that?" He wanted us to say he was right. He always got what he wanted.

"I'll make them disappear," Dad said. "But you have to change the name of your band. You have to change your look. You have to listen to me from now on."

Why did *we* always have to change? Why couldn't the world change instead?

We didn't know Dad could hack. If that's what he did. He wouldn't let us watch.

He created a computer code to erase every trace of us in cyberspace. At least that's what we told our friends. They said, with that kind of skill, why didn't he become one of those software hotshots who retired, a millionaire, by thirty?

We couldn't say because Dad wasn't a normal human being. Because when we asked how he did what he did, all he said was, "Magic."

"The shoe make the man," Ya-Ya liked to say. We slipped into our birthday patent leather Mary Janes. And became, simply, the Twins.

Not long after we lost our shot at fame, Dad lost his job at the plant. He wasn't the only one. "It's like a disease," Mom said. "It started when you were little. The robots taking over. Remember when I tried to get my job back at the bank?"

First tellers had become obsolete. Assembly line workers. Cashiers. Receptionists. Travel agents. Bakers. Warehouse workers. Even some therapy animals: our science teacher told us someone invented mechanical harp seals for Alzheimer's patients.

Dad said he would sue to get his job back. Couldn't stand by and do nothing when the whole city was getting the blood sucked right out of it.

"Who you going to sue, the Japanese," we asked, "for making their cars so good?"

At that, he flew into our room. We closed our door so the daycare babies wouldn't see and shut the windows so the neighbors wouldn't hear. Then he flung from our shelves all our framed photos and artwork. Our retro turntable and LPs. Our rainbow bracelets with glass beads. He ripped up lyrics from our favorite bands, which we had taped all over the walls. He threw Day of the Dead mirrors and nail polish bottles at us when we tried to stop his rampage. He dropped our heaviest books on our stocking feet. "Out!" he said and shoved us when we wouldn't obey.

We listened outside our closed door, ears to wood, as he shattered our treasures. "Don't go in," Mom whispered. We said nothing more and waited him out, like a storm. "You don't know what he's capable of," she said, then slunk away.

But we did. We had overheard Ya-Ya's words at Papu's funeral: Dad killed his own father. You never forget your first memories. Especially when Dad was helpful enough to remind us, now and then, what he was really like.

Minutes or hours later, we picked up the cracked glass and let it pierce our skin. We tripped on shards, and blood soaked our socks. We sucked the thick liquid from our fingertips, pretending to be vampires.

At dinner, all we did was swallow and scrape our plates. We nudged Mom to stand up for us, for once, as she had promised she would.

"Honey," she said, in a long drawl, like a dribble from a spoon. She swayed toward him, her freshly made mouth quivering. "Of course you're upset. But the girls—"

"I'll buy them anything they want once I get another job. You too, babe." He knelt beside Mom's chair and buried his face in her lap. "A house with *two* bathrooms," he promised. "A diamond ring to match the sparkle in those goddess eyes."

We looked away from them and at each other but still had to hear the kissing and cooing that curdled the milk in our half-empty glasses.

19
---

*H*e never kept those promises.

And Mom was wrong. We did know what Dad was capable of, which is why we killed him. We had to protect ourselves. No one else did.

That's what everyone says on those crime shows.

Which doesn't mean it's not true.

The brick wall couldn't move no matter how hard it was pushed, and apparently, neither could we. The snow swirled and spooked, hypnotizing us. We were getting sleepy, the way people do, we had heard, in the moments before frostbite.

20

We saw ourselves walking to our babysitting job that night, passing the shells of abandoned houses. Front yards tall with crabgrass. The smell of cooked-up cough syrup and singed hair. We could measure how long a neighbor had been laid off from the height of the pokeweed choking the shrubs.

We fed the kids their plain macaroni, gave them a bath, squeezing blue degreasing dish soap into the water, and read *Go to Sleep, Groundhog* to them in bed. We turned off the light half an hour early, hoping they wouldn't know the difference. We had biology to do.

The big sister climbed out of bed first. "I need a drink of water."

The little brother trudged out to the living room. "You didn't kiss me good night."

We stroked their backs and carried them to bed. Then they said:

"You need to stay with me and pet my hair."

"You need to hold my hand, or I'll have nightmares."

"I can't sleep without music."

"I can't sleep unless there's no sound at all."

We patted them and played the ukulele we always carried in our backpack. We waited for their slow breath to arrive, for the tiny wheezes to escape their noses. We tiptoed out, and then the little brother said, "I only sleep in the day."

His big sister said, "We turn into bats at night."

We stomped back to their rooms. "Not. One. More. Word. Or else."

They exhaled, and it sounded like snuffling back tears, but we told ourselves it was only sleepy breath. Our yelling erased the words from the groundhog book we had read to them so sweetly. All they would recall were our threats. We said, "You get out of bed again, and you're grounded. For the rest of your sad little lives." Then we slammed the bedroom doors.

They were silent for the rest of the night. When Dad hollered at us and used those same words, we had never dared talk back, either.

What had we become? Or, rather, who? We covered our eyes so we wouldn't have to look at each other.

21

*T*hen.

   And now.

But finally we let ourselves see. We lifted our eyelids, tenting hands over foreheads so we could look at each other through the static of snow. We punched each other's biceps. "See what he did? He made us hard." If that wasn't enough to indict him, what was?

We shivered some heat back into our veins. We wriggled to let the blood flow. We weren't ready to leave quite yet.

One of us said, "It's better to be soft?" The fluffy snow squished under our heels. "No one was going to rescue us. Mom was worthless."

"Don't say that."

We didn't want to be mean. One of us, at least. Anyway, who said we needed rescuing? We weren't like his pathetic tow truck customers.

22

The day Dad sold the Bull, Mom asked him how we would practice for our road test when he traded in our only vehicle for a tow truck.

We wondered the same thing, but we just said what we knew he wanted to hear. "Epic." At least he had a job. If we didn't give him lip, we still thought he might even pay us back for all the treasures he had broken, over the years, in our room.

Mom, still in her daycare uniform, sunflower T-shirt and hair pulled back in a scarf, waved him off. She washed her hands over and over. She did that blinky thing with her eyes that made her look like an alien, zinging around the living room, stacking errant blocks the daycare babies had knocked over. "We can't . . ."

But Dad was already opening the passenger door, beckoning us outside. We saw him through the kitchen window, in work boots, jeans, and short sleeves despite the cold. He had trimmed his beard and hair for the occasion, which begged for pictures. We grabbed our new phones—hard-earned through nights and weekends at Downriver Chik-N—short down coats, and stocking caps. We dashed outside, took photos of him and his new truck, then climbed in.

The truck was a tank, a whale, a mountain. Every bit as big as he was. Bright yellow letters rose up on the cab, embellished with thunderbolts: "Moose Tows."

At dinner, Mom asked how he paid for it.

He uncrossed his legs. Leaned back, the way he didn't let us, lifting the chair on two legs. Leaned forward again. Then said he had mortgaged the house.

Mom stopped swirling her fork in mashed potatoes, stopped pretending she was eating them. She left the table without another word and buried herself in bubble bath.

We didn't know much about mortgages. If we lost the house, we figured we could always find another, maybe a better one, with two bathrooms so we wouldn't have to hold it in every time Mom decided to soak herself. Dad had been out of work for a whole year. At least now he would be out of the house, too.

The tow truck was better than a job on some shitty factory floor. He was his own boss. An entrepreneur. Mom didn't need to drive, since her daycare babies came to her. He said all this in the smoothest voice, the one he used to make her purr. He sat next to her while we pretended to do our homework. He stroked her pulse point under the ear, and she closed her eyes and sucked in her lips. He cupped her chin, stroked her down to the clavicle.

She said, "Mmmm . . ." He pushed his chair closer and lifted her legs over his knees. She leaned into him, now soft as rain.

But in the darkest part of the night, once we all lay in bed, we heard him say, loud as hail, "I can't take it back.

Dad took us for rides through blizzards, when no one else dared venture out. "Now you know why I love Alaska," he said as we sped over dirt roads and asphalt, concrete and slippery side streets. "This is like riding on the back of a moose." Between customers, he taught us how to shift gears and steer, how to pump brakes on ice and always check our blind spots.

The tow truck was the Batmobile and Santa's sleigh. In it we flew through the thickest, stickiest weather. We dredged up flimsy cars and even 4 × 4s fallen into ditches. We pulled and salvaged poor schmucks begging for help.

We felt sorry for them—a mother with a toddler whose car had given up the ghost on the roadside. We berated them mercilessly. "Oh, help me, Moose! I drove too fast and went in the ditch!"

Moose Tows made money, too, while it lasted—before Dad's road rage turned his customers away. Enough to treat us and Rex to burgers and fries at the drive-through. Enough, apparently, to buy fried chicken for strangers.

In other words, too much.

We stared so long we burnt the whole tray.

Dad and a boy, all gangly limbs like an octopus, had appeared in the dining room at Downriver Chik-N. We hid in the kitchen, where we could watch without being watched. Dad must have forgotten we worked here full time now, the summer before senior year.

They ordered biscuits. The cashier said they would have to wait for the next batch.

"You burn them, you buy them," our boss told us, dumping into the trash our once-tender lumps turned hard.

They ordered chicken, too. We watched them lick and suck. Fingers, bone, and skin. Extra-crispy and spicy, every last cranny, their tongues and lips so loud they drowned out the crackling of the deep-fry fat, all the way back in the kitchen. We swore we heard them lick each other's fingers, but now, half our lives later, we couldn't be sure that was true.

"Who's the kid?" we asked each other. His big eyes and sharp chin looked familiar. His face, statue smooth, unmarred by even a minor infestation of acne. With such clear skin, he should have been in a movie. Maybe he was. Yes, that must be where we had seen him before. On the big or small screen, in a magazine—that's what we wanted to believe.

He was more our age than Dad's. Should have been our friend, not his. If that's what he was.

He wore Dad's baseball cap backwards. His favorite, the one he never let us wear, with a cartoon of a moose.

Dad was smooth shaven, biceps glistening, his white wifebeater pocked with sweat. He was slimmer, more boyish than we had ever seen. He paid for Octopus's food. Our lunch was always deducted from our paychecks.

We wiped our own sweat from our hairnets and pulled up the sagging elastic-waist pants of our brown polyester uniforms.

Their arms brushed each other's. The boy hovered closer to Dad than he should have. Not that middle-aged guys didn't try to sidle up to us. All the time. Sugar leeched out of our gum and left our tongues dry.

Dad could be bi. We had thought we were too, at twelve. Sometimes still did. Just because we hadn't heard about him having affairs after Pixie didn't mean he wasn't.

Maybe Octopus Boy was Octopus Man. People often said our friend Haley's mom looked like she was her sister.

We held our stomachs to keep the food from rising up. The buzzer rang, and we pulled the new biscuits from the oven. The cashier offered them to Dad and Octopus Boy, who sat in a corner next to the window. Steam floated from plates. They buttered for each other, even dripped the same honey pouch and licked their fingers, then bit into the flesh of the flaky food we had baked.

It seemed illicit, watching them. Like hovering over a first date, unseen. Listening to someone talking in his sleep, spilling the name of a bad crush—a teacher or best friend's boyfriend. Eavesdropping on a stranger vomiting her dinner into a plastic bag as you walked by her car. Looking through the trees when someone squatted in the woods. There are things we avert our eyes to. Or should.

That night we told Mom we had seen Dad with a teen at Downriver Chik-N. She was boiling water for pasta, dangling her face over the hot pot to open pores. She didn't turn around when we started to talk.

"Must be helping with odd jobs," she said, into the steam.

"How odd?" we asked.

Nothing.

Then we hovered on each side of her and repeated our question. Maybe she just hadn't heard us before.

Her only response was to lower her face so far we thought she might jump in.

23

At sixteen, we had been old enough to take care of ourselves. Old enough to drive. Old enough to marry. Old enough to have kids. Old enough to quit school. Old enough to do all the things our own parents had done at that age.

Even old enough to choose not to.

Now that we were almost twice that age, we finally saw how young we had been. What babies we were when we started turning our backs on Dad, what unformed things when we had decided we already knew enough. Now we were sure of less and less, each minute we lingered here in the funeral snow.

That's what one of us said, with her eyes. The other just spoke with a single middle finger.

The clouds yawned. Sparks crackled from the sky and tingled our lungs as we breathed them in.

We were old enough and smart enough now not to try to punch the brick church wall we leaned against. Instead we dug a hole in the snow with our boots and punched the frozen grass. The earth puckered for a moment, then settled into an indent the shape of our fists. We were finally as strong as Dad. We could tell because the dents we left were now as big as his.

24

We gave each other back massages and foot rubs. We nitpicked each other's hair and cascaded it into fish tails, double-Dutch braids, and French twists. We knocked knees and locked hips, offered fist bumps and high fives. We pulled out our sister's splinters and painted her nails, black with gold tips. We were girls, so we were allowed to touch. The boys at school stiffened next to each other, swayed to opposite sides, even if they were brothers.

But touching each other felt too much like touching ourselves. What we needed was a foreign body. Preferably with a fringe of stubble on his chin and a curve in his spine like a question mark.

"You're so lucky," people told us. "You never have to be lonely. You always have each other."

How could we make them understand? That the two of us together only made one whole person. That they, the singletons, were the lucky ones. They never split in half.

We longed for someone we hadn't yet met. Someone we couldn't share with our twin but still had to. The calculus was too complicated. So we shrouded ourselves in oversized hoodies and pretended not to look at boys.

Yet the crushes came. On the boy we called Superhero because he drew comics of giant insects with special powers. The one we called Hair, who sang in the high school musical dressed in drag. Weatherman, who looked like an emo version of a TV meteorologist. Two came backstage on talent night after we played, a sprinkle of stubble on their chins, just the faintest hint of manhood. One: hair pulled back, except for a wayward curl across the forehead. The same band shirt we loved to wear to bed, with nothing but our tiny panties. The other: a suit, his signature look, paired with a form-fitting black T-shirt and red high-tops. These boys gifted us with M&M's, then watched us bite into the green ones.

We watched them chew the reds with their sharp canines. We all sucked the other colors, warm chocolate busting from the shell and sliding down our throats. Blood rushed around in all the right places. Our breath steamed in front of our hands. We reached for more candy, and our short tops slid up, exposing slivers of belly—one hard, one tender. We followed the boys' eyes as they chose which one they wanted.

We loved the smell of their skin, briny the way we imagined ocean air, though we had only ever been to freshwater lakes. We loved the oily musk of their hair, the branches of their bodies dangling off chairs, the way they flexed their fingers over pens, ferocious and focused. We loved the look of their shoulders and clavicles and eye-brows, but we didn't love these boys. How could we? They didn't know our secrets. We didn't know theirs. We twins were so inseparable, it was impossible to be alone with a boy long enough to call him our boyfriend.

Weatherman and Superhero didn't care. "Call us what-ever you want," they said. "Just don't stop doing what you're doing."

By that time, junior year, we were hooking up. In the janitor's closet, a sub shop restroom or alley, behind the lilac bush in the schoolyard, we bit our lips to squelch the sound of release. Buttons, zippers, panties, bras, jock straps slipped off under bleachers and dark viaducts.

We weren't the Slutty Twins anymore, we told our-selves. We had held back so long. We weren't going all the way. We were just playing around. Conducting an experi-ment, to see if we could separate, a few moments at a time, from our twin.

We coupled off, but only for a few minutes, the time it took to walk home from school. We kissed, we rubbed, we stroked. We could say stop and go, yes and no. Until we didn't.

We were so smart. We weren't having sex yet. That's what we said.

No one had warned us how easy it could be to slip from hands and lips to thrusting hips. We had been told to stay in control. That we could choose which body parts we wanted where, border police blocking prospective immigrants. No one told us what to do if we *wanted* to let them in. To prove we were human, not Artemis and Apollo. Not a family with secrets so awful we couldn't have sleepovers and wear short shorts when Mom was afraid the neighbors might see our bruises.

So one day, on the way home from school, one of us took a detour. One of us let her boy lead her up the porch steps, through the door, down the hallway to his room. No time for slipping under the covers. *No time like the present.* Did he really say that, in his perfect-mimic weatherman voice, even though he was wearing soccer shorts, for a change, that showed off his bulging cross-country runner's thighs? That day, sun bright, shades pulled, one of us could not help saying yes. *Right there, just like that, yes, don't stop. Just be gentle, it only hurts a little. No, it's OK. Yes, my first time. What are you doing? Don't be a tease. Like that. A little slower. Yes. Oh yessssss.* The sound of air whistling out of a tire. The inability to move, even lift a chin from the pillow. *My sister, though. My sister will worry. Gotta go.*

Only at dinner, looking at Mom over the top of a glass of milk, did we wonder if this was how it happened before we were born. If this was how we were conceived, on a walk home from high school. If we were why she had never finished.

But we weren't her. She didn't even know we were here, on our way to a tour of the University of Michigan. We didn't tell her, because we didn't want her to say we didn't have enough money, with a second mortgage on the house and the tow truck business tanking.

It was the fall of senior year when Mr. Haddad, our orchestra teacher, took us for a ride. We twins sat in the backseat in turtlenecks and ballerina buns. We didn't wear his hat or let our arms swish against him. We didn't want to be like Octopus. To have people think we were letting an old man take advantage of us. You never knew who was watching.

Our teacher couldn't believe we had never been to a college campus before. No one in our family believed in college, we explained. He laughed at that. "It exists," he said. "I'll show you."

We meant we didn't think college was for people like us, we said, people whose dad drove a truck, whose mom let her daycare money disappear almost as soon as she was paid. We couldn't even afford the application fees.

We were new to Ann Arbor, too. After forty-five minutes in Mr. Haddad's purple Ford Focus, we arrived at an alternate universe filled with people like us. We didn't know yet what that meant.

College students spilled out onto the Diag, the convergence of three sidewalks surrounded by grass. Some of them lounged outside UGLI, the undergrad library. Some students talked philosophy. Some spoke foreign languages. Some smoked hash, and no one snitched. Some of them stared at a man who paced, reciting the Greek alphabet. Some gathered around the art museum, playing jaw harps or guitars. We leaned toward them, magnetized. "You should have brought your instruments," our teacher said.

The bell tower caroled the hour. We passed the Women's League and the Student Union, ivy covered. Trees and shaded benches. Mr. Hadadd pointed out the Calder statue. Some of the students danced around it. We had never seen anything like it before. The dancing or the statue, which seemed to dance, too. We sisters held hands and shimmied with each other.

Some of the students sang in acapella groups. We joined in. No one laughed at us, as they would have in high school.

"Still think college is not for people like you?" Mr. Hadadd asked.

We belted out the next tune, hitting each high note.

He had arranged for us to sit in on a strings class taught by his former professor. Why he did us these favors, we tried not to wonder. He didn't stare at the skin on our arms, up our shoulders, or all the way down our necks. He ignored our freshly shaved bare legs under sunny yellow skirts.

In the classroom, the professor breathed fire, and the music broiled. We loved Mr. Hadadd, but his class was nothing like this. Trills and staccato, loud gashes of vibrato. Fingers swept from one octave to the next without bridges between. We could feel the bows stroking our bellies, almost. We were the cellos. Basses, violas, violins. We were catgut and horsehair, the trees from which the wood was carved. The varnish that made it all shine. The music became us. We belonged here.

At the end of class, Mr. Hadadd introduced us to his old professor. "My two best students," he said.

We didn't think of ourselves that way. Dad always said we weren't like other people, but now we were too old to believe in the tales he told. Our blip of YouTube fame felt like something he had conjured up, too. Since then, we had sensed our power leaking from our bodies like our monthly menses. We didn't know there was anywhere we could go to replenish it again.

Now we knew. This was home.

Back in the Focus, Mr. Hadadd told us to quit our jobs and concentrate on schoolwork for our senior year. If we kept up our grades, we would be accepted, he said. Without a job, though, how would we pay?

"Financial aid," he said. The two most beautiful words.

We always menstruated in sync, but then, one day, one of us missed. We watched the plus sign materialize on the pink stick stained with pee, and now we knew: We *were* women. Human. Because this is what women can do: We carry bodies in our bodies. Clusters of cells, multiplying. We generate, procreate.

Mom made a plan right away, that night, never so quick and sure, never willing before to hide something from Dad. Her little body could not possibly hold all that adrenaline. Usually, it was filled with what she called "nerves," but this was the opposite. No finger biting or feet jiggling, just minimal movement, *Here, here, here, let's get this done.* Her beauty mark pulsed with energy. She called her Sunflower clients to say she would be closed the next day. *Family emergency.* Then Ya-Ya: Could she borrow the car in the morning? *A birthday surprise, please don't tell Moose.*

So late, yet Dad had still not come home. She admitted, for the first time, she didn't know where he was, where he always went. *Just as well.* For once, she didn't pace and peer out the window, a little dance she never seemed to know she was doing. That night, she tucked us in like invalids, but we didn't mind. She said, "Go to sleep, my two eyes and ears." With those words, we were five again. This time, though, could it be that she was the one trying to protect *us*?

In the morning, Mom tiptoed out of bed, not waking Dad. She lent us her cardigan sweaters and sensible shoes and pulled her hair into a tidy twist. She drove us to a clinic she found through a secret social media group and shielded us from gun-toters shouting us down on our way to the front door. Inside, she prepaid for the procedure with a stack of twenty-dollar bills from her customers. In a boxlike, stuffy medical room, one of us bristled at a shot of local anesthesia, swallowed a pill, and waited. Later, once she returned from the bathroom, we all could tell the other body inside her was gone.

She was deflated but also lighter. Smaller, though she would never be as small as she had once been. There was no undoing this. She would not let it undo her. And yet. Her lungs collapsed with each breath, her feet too heavy to lift.

"You deserve to make decisions about your own body," Mom said once we had returned home. This from the woman who made animal sounds behind the closed bedroom door at night, the back of her neck scratched up by morning, as if from a cat we didn't have.

Her voice, from years ago, echoed in our heads, back when Dad weighed her on the bathroom scale and said she was not as small as she once had been: *I was sixteen going on twelve. What did you expect?* Our age when she had married him.

Mom knew what to do. She threw her receipt in the

clinic's trash can. But at home, Dad saw the pain pills and asked what they were for. She said, "Appendicitis."

We, though, were careless. We left the post-procedure instructions on the table next to our beds. Dad found them and said, "I should have your tubes tied. You know, they do that with dogs."

Later, at dinner, forks scraped plates. Glasses spilled and no one bothered to wipe up the mess. Mom said nothing. All we could do was tap each other's thighs and breathe in sync.

"Girls." Dad broke the silence. "I had to get *girls*? The two of you don't add up to one boy."

He swore he would find the one who "did this" to us. Hunt him down. We knew word would spread. "Stay away from those twins with the crazy dad," people would say. We would never get close enough to touch a superhero or a weatherman again.

When we were little, Dad wouldn't let us *into* the house unless the temperature dropped below freezing. Now he wouldn't let us *out*, all month, except for school. We couldn't even babysit. "You're lucky I don't ground you both for the rest of your sad little lives for lying," he said.

We balled our fists and vowed to teach him a lesson. "When he's old and needs a ride to the hospital, we'll say, 'You mean the vet?'"

He punished Mom, too, for covering up for us. He confiscated her credit card.

We would take her with us, we said, when we left home for good.

Just as Granny had said we should, so many years ago.

The next fall we packed our bags. Dad could never ground us again. He could never again lock us out of the house all night in the cold and force us to sleep in a tent or a snow fort. Yell at us from his truck to cover our butts. Break all our mirrors and trinkets in a rage.

But he could still hurt Mom. Still make her squeal behind the bedroom door. Still confiscate her bank card. Unless we brought her with us.

So we lugged a bag up from the basement for Mom. We could hide her in our dorm room. Once we were sophomores, we could rent an apartment with a room for her. No one would ever punish her for helping us again.

But she stayed.

The biggest mystery of all was this: When we asked why, all she said was, "I love him." The three most useless words.

If loving him meant putting up with his shit, we were done. We never had to talk to him again.

As a parting gift, Mom gave us a velvet box containing the famous diamond studs. The ones we had seen on Pixie that day at the shoe store. The box Dad had given to Mom after their big fight. We each took one and slid the post through the hole, fastened it tight, wore it always.

Then all we could do was pile our bags in the belly of the Greyhound bus, ride it out to I-94, and go west.

We left without her.

25

*W*as that it?" we asked each other. "That's when we decided to cut him off?"

"Did *we* decide?"

"What's that mean?"

Our toes were freezing in our funeral shoes. We stomped to make heat and kicked each other's shins.

"We couldn't protect her," we said.

"She didn't want us to."

"We abandoned her."

"She wouldn't come."

"We could have fit her inside our suitcase. She was almost that small."

"Then we would have been as bad as him."

"What else could we have done?"

"Fight or flight."

"And if we had fought, someone would have gotten hurt."

"As if no one did."

"We went to college. Grew up."

"Then why are we hovering here, stuck at seventeen?"

We stuffed our hands behind each other's necks for warmth. We leaned against the wall and each other. We stretched our backbones long enough to remind us that we had them.

"Can't we go back inside? There's no evidence left."

"There's the rest of our lives."

"Without Dad."

"He's not the one on trial here."

"Then who is?"

But we knew.

For the first time that endless evening, we actually agreed. And only on one thing: we had been collecting evidence, all right, but not against Dad.

The defendant in this case was *us*.

Part Two

26

All freshmen at U of M had to share a dorm. Of course, we chose to room with each other.

We became Wolverines. Members of our hall, our class, our school. Or tried to.

We played icebreaker games at orientation but opted out of Two Truths and a Lie. We danced with a drink in each hand at frat parties, only to find, at the end of our favorite song, that our cups had spilled on our feet. We read about the lives of other freshmen on social media. We heard them complain in the cafeteria and watched them on the Diag.

Some of them were used to privacy, they said, and resented their roommates' music or perfume so much they spent their afternoons in the library and their evenings in the lounge. Some were stuck with girls who couldn't keep down their Jell-O shots, and, even after they laundered their sheets, the air in their rooms still reeked. Some found a new best friend, a crush, or even a mate in a random housing match. Some missed sleeping with their dogs and imagined their roommates covered with fur. Some were paired with boys who had never washed their own clothes before and who let their T-shirts sour with a cocktail of sweat, Coke, and ketchup.

We couldn't have imagined not sleeping in the same room. Even the distance between our beds, no longer stacked bunks, sent cold wind through our blankets and made us sometimes roll off our mattresses and warm our hands in each other's bedtime braids.

Some freshmen had blue hair. Some had shaved heads or bedheads. Some had pink skin or brown skin or black skin or black-and-blue skin.

Some, like us, had tattoos. We wore our eighteenth birthday presents to each other on the insides of our thumbs. The opening parenthesis on one of us, the closing on the other.

Some freshmen, we heard, had been fed bacon at every meal at home, and they rebelled by turning vegan. Some had grown up on slow food and became microwave pizza-terians. Some had relied on food stamps and now picked out of the cafeteria's salad bar only the most expensive items, like pine nuts and raspberries.

Some grew up in the city, and they clutched their purses close to their bodies or planted their wallets and phones deep in the security of their front pockets. Some arrived from the country, and when they left their laptops on the study carrels, they were surprised to find them gone when they returned from a quick trip to the bathroom.

The first thing every freshman did, we later found out,

before deciding who they trusted and didn't, who might sleep with or tell on them, who might know all the answers and who might ask them to cheat, before telling each other where they were from and what their parents did or didn't do, before even finding out each other's names, was find someone to sit with at lunch. For real? Sometimes it did seem just like high school.

Some were from Grosse Pointe and had the boat club memberships to prove it. Some, from Birmingham or Bloomfield Hills, wore Bermuda shorts. Some were from Hamtramck or Ecorse or the wrong side of Eight Mile, and they reflexively locked every door behind them and always carried a compact canister of pepper spray in their pockets or purses. Some of them were from Traverse City or other points north and had packed an arsenal of winter coats and high-tech electric blankets. Some of them were from the Upper Peninsula and spoke about the joys of ice fishing with a brisk accent that reminded us of clear Canadian air. Some were from Flint and didn't like it when people asked if their mothers had drunk the city water when they were pregnant.

Some had graduated from boarding schools like Cranbrook or prep schools like New Country Day and displayed their debate team trophies shamelessly on dressers. A few had gone to public schools like ours (though it took us months to find them), where popular kids trolled the halls spray-painting lockers in plain sight.

Most of them were singletons. None of them was one of us. But we would keep looking.

Some had come from outside the state. Some (not many) from California. Some from Virginia. *Only virgins live in Virginia*, we used to say, sitting in the elbow of our pear tree, inflating condoms from middle school health class. Now we couldn't hear the name of the state without eyeing each other and giggling behind cupped hands.

Some freshmen had come from other countries—Korea and China and India. Countries we would have traded limbs to visit if anyone had asked us to.

While we played foosball with our hallmates, we wondered, Would we like this new group of kin? Would we love them? More than our old one? Haley and Nevaeh hadn't gone to college. We had said we would text them every day, but now that we had left them and our former life behind, we couldn't think what to say.

Some of the freshmen in our hall complained about their dirty laundry, the dirty bathrooms. (They wondered aloud if that was how their moms spent Saturdays—doing laundry, cleaning toilets?) Most complained hardest about the slowness of the internet and the weakness of the cafeteria coffee.

They complained about the noise of their complaining.

But we were secretly happy, because the freedom to speak our minds was a new pleasure. No one listened in and threatened, "You want me to give you something worth whining about?"

Each room housed two of everything. We were used to sharing a desk and a dresser and a closet. Our beds were made for sturdy eighteen-year-olds. At home we had slept in the same ones since we had graduated from cribs. Our college-issued mattresses were stained with what was likely menstrual blood, but we imagined, instead, that they were darkened by longing. To find someone as strange as we were, to touch more than skin, to finally tell all. We still tossed in the night, trapped in a tangle of sheets, our eyelids stuck shut and mouths open wide as the sky.

Some freshmen dreamed of inventing a computer that could invent another computer. Our fantasies leaned toward recording contracts and Grammys. Of Granny's disembodied voice saying, from our phone, "Finally, you ran away from home."

We dreamed we were back in our brown-shagged house, plugging our ears against Mom's squeals and Dad's roars, which we didn't yet understand.

Yet? Who were we kidding?

We dreamed of Dad cheating on Mom and Mom never cheating on her diet. We woke choking on our snores. Our ribs caved in. Our flesh disappeared. We almost evaporated. In the dark, we mistook ourselves for Mom and cried out so shrilly, our resident assistant knocked on our door. "You OK in there?"

Often, we were jolted by a violent storm and forgot it wasn't Dad. We rolled off our beds to check on Mom, then remembered we had gone and she had stayed behind.

Was she sleeping now? Was she dreaming of the freedom she had given to us but would not grant herself? Did she secretly envy us our distance? Was she dreaming of us dreaming of her? We took careful notes during all our classes, so we could teach her everything we were going to learn without her.

Some freshmen were orphans or half orphans. We just pretended we were.

We wondered if we would fit in. Some freshmen were descended from a long line of college-educated people. All, we often imagined, except us.

Girls like us didn't deserve the best university in the state. Did they? They didn't belong in Advanced Studio Orchestra their freshman year, but there we were. Letting the sawing of our bows sing the longing we couldn't articulate with our mouths, as we held the notes so long our arms hurt. We took music theory tests, which made us feel more official and less special at the same time. As if our professor—the brilliant musician who had taught Mr. Haddad a generation ago—were taking the skim and the fat and turning us all into homogenized milk.

We lived on a two-person island that resembled a college dorm room.

Finally free to choose what to study, a few freshmen secretly wished, we suspected, that someone would tell them exactly what to do. We sometimes did.

Some freshmen had grown up in neighborhoods where

drive-by shootings were as common as drive-through drugstores. Some had lived in public housing. Some still lived in their own private worlds.

Some had lived within minutes of university hospitals. Some had watched neighbors bleed to death before an ambulance arrived. We were from somewhere in between, right across the city border—not the well-scrubbed suburbs or their opposite. We had always thought we were middle class, but so did those with summer homes. If they were in the middle, where were we?

Some had gone to high schools that would later be decimated by a lone shooter's rampage. They were lucky to have been born early enough to miss it, but they didn't know that at the time.

Some had been shot at because of the color of their skin. Some had been attacked because they were trans. Some were told they were too ghetto to get into college. Some freshmen were going to hell, everyone said. Some of them had already tried, with needles, pills, or razors.

We kept searching—on the Diag, on social media, in the cafeteria. Hoping to see *some of them* turn into *some of us*. We painted our lips Red Delicious. We flipped our hair and dug fingers into our cheeks, pretending we had dimples. We fetched Frisbees thrown too far off the lawn. When the player who hadn't caught the Frisbee ran away without a word of thanks, we buried our heads in our U of M hoodies.

Boys liked us, but we rebuffed the attention of *those kinds* of boys, the ones who saw only our long necks and goddess hair. Other boys? We never would have imagined we intimidated them. With what? Our height or speed? We didn't know why a few girls approached and then slunk off, why most girls stayed away.

Did we seem too coupled, too self-sufficient, our twin codes too hard to read? Back then we just figured we were strange, like Dad. Maybe we hadn't really left him behind. Maybe when our shadow fell across the Diag, it was shaped like his.

We shuffled into our freshman seminar. We wore jean jackets, leggings, and tall brown riding boots. The other ten students wore hoodies, soccer shorts, skinny jeans. Scuffed Chucks or dainty flats with bows. We all sat at a long table, the spiffy bow-tied professor among us, not even at the head. "Let's go around and introduce ourselves," he said, in either a Canadian or a fake British accent. "First name. Where you're from. What pronoun you go by."

Most chose the usual—he or she. Sometimes the choice matched our guess, sometimes not. Then one student— with a face like a Halloween crescent moon (the most striking in the room)—made throat-clearing noises for several seconds. "Staver. Grosse Pointe (a suburb of Detroit). And please—say 'They.'"

"OK." The professor nodded more times than necessary and jiggled his pointy black leather shoes with red laces, but he remained matter of fact, like a waiter taking sandwich orders.

We two scanned the table for the other half of the twin set but could find no second crescent moon. "They" was one guy. Or girl. Or both in one body.

We had always thought of ourselves as plural, but no one had asked us before. Then our turn came and we chose our pronoun. "We." We had always wanted to.

"Both of you?" the professor asked.

"Of course." Maybe he didn't understand what the word meant. Or maybe we were wrong. We parsed the small print on the syllabus until our eyes hurt.

After class, we caught up with the other misfit pronoun on the way to the cafeteria. They were taller than us but just as slim. Short kinky hair with a glint of blue, the same color as their mascara. An Adam's apple we couldn't stop staring at. A credit-card-sized tattoo on their forearm that reminded us of a painting we must have seen on a postcard or at the Detroit Institute of Arts.

"Hey, Staver."

"Hey," they said.

In the cafeteria we picked out the salad bar gems, grape leaves and hearts of palm. Staver heated frozen pizza in the microwave. "If you don't mind my asking," they said, "are you gender fluid, too?"

We wanted to be, if it meant being like them. Confident about their otherness. We had always known that who we were was a slippery thing. We tapped each other's thighs, which meant *This one's a keeper.* We told each other, with the touch of skin to fingertips, that now that we had left our parents' house, we were finally home. But we didn't know how to answer Staver's actual question.

"Nonbinary? Gender neutral? Genderqueer?" they asked.

Our faces hung blank.

"Do you know what those terms mean?"

We had heard of them but wanted to hear more. We plugged our mouths with a grape leaf each and pretended we would have lots to say if only we could talk.

"Do you want to know?"

Our heads bobbed up and down.

"Pretend this is a box for girls. This is a box for boys." They gestured with each hand. "What happens if you don't fit in either box? Or if sometimes you're in one, sometimes in the other? Or what if gender is like a house? You spend time in more than one room, right? For some people it's more like clothes. One day you wear this" — they pointed to their pinstripe vest over an untucked collared shirt — "sometimes you wear that." We followed their head to a girl at the next table in a strappy sundress.

Staver continued to lecture us, gesticulating with their pizza, the pucks of pepperoni slipping on the grease. The flash seminar on gender and identity theory lasted till the cafeteria closed and we had to invite Staver back to our dorm.

They had a friend named Sebastian, who was also in our class. Staver texted him, and he arrived to help us push the beds together and stream *Orlando* while we drank through fat straws the bubble tea Sebastian had brought. Staver strummed our ukulele. We knew then they were one of us, even if we couldn't have foreseen they would be the best man/maid of honor combined at our wedding.

Sebastian had the most symmetrical face we had ever seen, two twin halves, together round as a MoonPie. His part sliced his scalp right down the middle. He was balance incarnate. Long hair but broad shoulders. Tight pants but loose shirt, unbuttoned further than we had ever dared, even as the Slutty Twins. Wound-up curls but smooth skin, browner than ours. Shoulders back, head up when he walked; but a soft springy slump when he sank down in a chair, his ear turned toward us, mouth closed, eyes open so wide the lids disappeared. A face without hair, but a chest furnished with a delicious patch of fur. He was what we would paint if we could paint (and suddenly we burned to do it). We told him things we had never told even our best friends, and he nodded his head and said nothing. Hummed an earthy yogic *om*. A hand beckoned us to tell more. Then he plucked yarn from his pocket and wove us slender orange friendship bracelets matching his own.

We had always thought boys were all Mouth and Dick. But we would have painted him as an Ear. His fingers, long and slender as the Mona Lisa's. Would they feel cold and tingly on our backs or hot on our hips? Maybe he was nonbinary, too, like his friend. We didn't care. We wanted to be, too, if it meant this: a body made of contradictions and parallels. We wanted whatever he had. We both did, but we would share. Somehow. He carried a pocketknife and carved our likenesses from empty coffee cups and Styrofoam to-go plates, objects we had carelessly tossed in the trash. We each wanted to believe the picture he made of us was the best.

After the next class, Sebastian invited us to his own dorm to study. Staver brought a study partner, too, a boy named Cline. We loved his soft voice and asymmetrical hair. A boomerang and an antique mandolin hung on the walls. The ceiling was dotted with glow-in-the-dark stars. Sebastian's roommate, Colson, had a face as rounded as ours was sharp, a scratchy voice, and short dreads. He offered us grog. That's what he called his concoction in a steaming mug. All the other students we had met so far only drank Coke or beer.

One of us stared. One of us said, with our eyes, that

Sebastian was nothing compared to Colson, who moved like a dancer. Like a high-wire artist. He was made of steam. We could see right through him. Or was it smoke? We had never met anyone before who seemed to float more than walk. He could adapt to anything, we could tell, by the way he pretzeled his fingers around a pencil.

He had a superpower we couldn't name. Perhaps he could walk on the snow without falling in. Or maybe he could see what people hid behind their eyes. Since as long as we could remember we had been looking for boys—or girls—as slippery and strange as us. We should have known: we had to leave home to find them.

How did one of us know Colson was the one? How did we know how to breathe? To go back to sleep when we woke up in the middle of the night? To open our eyes to the sun?

Not just one of us wanted Colson. But one of us wanted him more.

We looked these boys over, temples to toes, not sure what we were looking for. And then we knew. We had found their tattoos, twin punctuation marks, a semicolon on each boy's palm, Colson's right, Sebastian's left.

"You know what it means?" Sebastian asked us. "It means pause."

Colson walked behind his friend and planted his hands on his shoulders, with a comfort we had never seen between boys.

We didn't need to know more once we knew they had marked themselves for each other. Just as we had.

They told us they had grown up together, in the same small town halfway between Detroit and Traverse City. "We're kind of like twins," Sebastian said.

"No, you're not."

"I'm black, you mean," Colson said. "And he's light brown."

"That's the least of it."

"Twins are so special?" Colson sat on his bed and patted a space for one of us to join him. He wore a flannel shirt and soccer shorts, a mix of sporty and hip. On his bare legs, his hair disappeared into the camouflage of his skin.

"When we were little, one day we switched clothes and pretended to be each other. Nobody knew we had swapped places," we said.

"Not even your parents?" Sebastian sat on his bed, his back against the wall, and one of us sidled up, to sit hip to hip.

"Even we forgot." We felt the boys' breath. We wanted to feel more. More what? We weren't thinking in words. Blood rushed between our legs, the way it had that day when we had wielded our gun and pointed it out the window. We shivered—one frightened, one thrilled. More power. We wanted more of this. Of these boys. Of what was in their mouths and on their skin.

"That's kind of creepy," they finally said.

"You have no idea."

Every day after class, the four of us studied together. Sometimes we were five, with Staver, or six, if Cline came, too. We twins went to health services and started swallowing birth control pills with our toast. Finally, one day, we paired off—boy-girl, boy-girl—on the two small beds.

We told Colson and Sebastian, "When you touch me, you touch her. Anything that happens to one of us, happens to both."

"Sounds kinky," Colson said.

"Not *physically*."

"Ooh, mysterious," Sebastian said.

We threw up our hands. "We're just warning you."

One of us walked our boy across campus, to our room, while the other stayed with her boy in his. Our boys dropped the blinds; we dimmed the lights.

In our two separate rooms, at the same time.

We wiggled out of our blue jean shorts and black tights, our semitransparent white tops stretched over bright-colored cotton camisoles. We removed our best panties, chosen for the occasion, with no blood stains or holes, then we slid under the covers in the narrow twin bed crammed against the wall. There was no room to lie next to each other, so one of us had to climb on top. They hesitated, so we went first. Turned out, we twins knew more than they did.

We each held our boy in our hands, then in our mouths. We slurped and gulped and hummed. We couldn't see our twin, but we sensed we were in sync. We wrapped our long dark hair around his sex and rubbed and strummed, the gesture not so different from playing guitar and singing along. Our thumbs so nimble, our throats so warm. They helped us with their hips, pressing us to thrust with our hands, then mouths, faster and faster.

And then we stopped. To linger, to lengthen the moment. To let them enter us, like a room. But first, to slip on a condom.

They fit inside our bodies the way air fills a room. All we wanted at that moment, which felt like our entire lives, was for them not to stop.

The springs squeaked, and we listened. Where had we heard that creaking before? Yes. The soundtrack of our childhood.

We pumped our hips and heard nothing more but the sound of our clenching, then our shivering. Our bodies went soft. We didn't mean to cry. What would our boys do if they saw? We hid our faces in our hair.

Then our boys cried, too. That's how we knew they were ours.

Each in her separate room, we made love for the first time. We had had sex before, quick and dirty, in cars and bathrooms. This was different.

Braided together with our boyfriends—which was what they now were—we spent the night apart for the first time. Yet we stayed twinned, knowing what the other had gone through. We tried not to wonder how long we would float, bodies linked to boys, brains to each other. We could double-date, but we couldn't be quadruplets.

Weeks passed, and we spent more time with Colson and Sebastian. We pulled their ears and nibbled them. We took the back of their hips, which they couldn't see, and molded them in the shape of our palms. They took *us* in their mouths and waited for us to push their heads away with our hands to signal we were done.

We pressed their temples like elevator buttons. We lifted and rocked their ankles. We let our hair sweep their cheeks. We blew bubbles and looked at their faces through them. We slipped lists into their pockets. We imprinted our creases onto theirs, and the pattern stuck. We walked in reverse so we could see their backs shrinking smaller and smaller. We dangled their legs in the crooks of our elbows and watched the knots in every muscle unbend. We rolled them across the floor and leapfrogged on top.

We wore their shirts, and they wore ours. We played guitar and sang for them, and they crumpled at our feet.

They rode their bikes to class, and we ran beside them, trying not to flaunt the fact that we were faster. They helped us with our homework, so we would ace the requirements for our meteorology class. We needed to prove, scientifically, that Dad didn't actually control the weather.

They lent us their earbuds and played music we didn't know we needed to hear. Afro punk, art punk, baroque pop. Coldwave and cow punk, crust core and dark cabaret. They played us emo and ethereal wave. Gypsy punk, grunge, geek rock, and indie folk. Math rock, Mod revival, Paisley Underground. Power pop, reggae, hip-hop, swamp pop, roots, and, finally, synth.

We talked futures. One wanted to teach, one wanted to fly. Their desires mixed with ours, in our heads and between our legs, so much we barely could tell ourselves apart.

On our pillows, they confessed their secrets. One: that he had kissed a boy. And liked it. And would do it again. The other: that he had killed a man.

We shucked off the covers and made for the door. Our throats filled with reflux, rusty metal down our pipes.

Then he laughed. "A joke."

We would tell them our secret. The big one, about Dad killing his dad. Which we decided, at that moment, was the real reason we didn't talk to him.

We really would tell our boys. Soon. That's what you did when you loved someone. That's how you *knew* you did.

We didn't go home for fall break, because Dad was there. We waited to visit Mom and Ya-Ya till we knew he was away on a hunting trip. We texted them every week. But when Dad tried to contact us, we ignored our phones.

27

When we moved to off-campus housing, the summer after freshman year, we unpacked only what we needed in our new lives. A few half-shirts would hold us till winter. Jeans ripped at the knees. Guitar, bass, ukulele. We didn't play the songs we had written for the Slutty Twins. The irony had been chased out of them.

The first thing we did was fill up the bathtub. We hadn't had one in the dorms. Now we could bury ourselves in bubbles whenever we needed to slow our pulse.

It was Staver who saw the ad on the bulletin board at the back of the Renaissance art history class they took with us. "Wanted: Models for life drawing. Great hourly rates." In hip coffee shops and old-school cafeterias, in the supermarket and on the dance floor, men kept telling us we looked like models. So what if they were feeding us a pickup line?

Staver answered the ad, too. With their crescent-moon face and slinky limbs, they were as luminous as paintings at the Detroit Institute of Arts, so no wonder they were hired by the same professor who hired us, for different days. Our only interest was the cash. Their parents provided an ample allowance, so we didn't understand why Staver took the job.

"It's the principle," they said.

"The principle of what?" we asked.

"Representation."

We scrunched up our mouths and waited, as we always did, for Staver to patiently explain.

"Nonbinary people need to be portrayed more often in art."

Of course. People like them, with Adam's apples and plucked eyebrows, with broad shoulders and soft skin, with slim waists and concave chests. Or other combinations that didn't have to be contradictions. Like so many people we saw on campus, now that we knew what to look for: Boys with bows in their long hair. Girls in leather jackets and motorcycle boots. Hadn't they opened our eyes to these things the first day we met?

When it was our turn in Life Drawing, we worked as a team. When one of us tired of holding a pose, the other resumed. The students hardly blinked. Did they see that one of us had a skinned knee, the other a birth mark on her left shoulder? Sometimes we wanted to scratch ourselves up, cut our skin in different places, just to test if anyone really saw us at all. They kept drawing our ears and hair, our eyes and thighs, as if we were one person.

Look, I'm the curvier one. My breasts are twice the size of hers, one of us wanted these art students to notice. *These abs? No small feat*, the other wanted all to see. But no one did.

We stifled sneers. *What a waste of attention.* We bit our index finger, the way Mom always did when she couldn't bring herself to say what she needed to say.

When fooling people is too easy, it's no longer fun. It was never meant to be fooling, anyway. More like dipping a finger in hot water to test the temperature.

Yet all those eyes also made our skin buzz. The hair on our arms tingle. The air run through our lungs.

One day, midpose, the AC blew out in the studio. Students started to sweat into their charcoal, turning it to mud. When our smooth skin puddled, the professor told everyone to go home. They could finish their drawings at the next class.

In the old house with the rickety wraparound porch that we rented with two other girls—the other half of our string quartet—the AC died, too. The grid had officially been overloaded on that record-hot day. To escape the heat, we wound our way to a shady place we knew, hidden deep in the woods near campus. We didn't invite our boyfriends or Staver, who tagged along so often, making our four-some into five. We wanted to skinny dip, just the two of us, naked as we were in the womb, swimming even then.

We wanted to cool our tempers. Why were we so riled up? Not just from the temperature.

But first we filled our pack with clementines and peanut butter crackers. Lemonade and a rifle. There could be bears out there. There could be men who didn't like it when we caught their pickup lines and threw them back.

We could have bought a pocket-size. Or even one disguised as a phone, if we had wanted to. Or a hands-free gun we could shoot just by swiveling our hips. But we were secretly proud of the nosy way the muzzle poked out, like a live thing. We had carried the rifle this far through our lives, and we were used to its heft. We wouldn't admit even to each other that we were still attracted to its power. No matter how hard we tried to run away from Dad, we brought him in our pack, thanks to ever looser open carry laws.

We had wrangled our hair into messy buns that tumbled out into high ponytails once we had raced each other to our favorite tree, the one that cooled the air like iced tea. We rolled in the grass and wove clover into each other's hair. We could breathe again. Out here, without the attention-pollution of the city, we could finally hear each other think. We inhaled the silence. It fed us.

Under a canopy of leaves, we fanned the backs of each other's necks with fresh-picked ferns. We peeled our fruit, stripped its membranes, then sucked out all the sweet juices. Refreshed, we bushwhacked further than we ever had, past twisted, prickly vines. Brambles tripped us, lodging thorns in thin skin, our hands reddening with overripe berries. We cursed our cuts. We ranted at each other. "Whose idea was it to come to this jungle?" "Who said this could beat the heat?"

And then we saw it. Not a mirage, but real water. We ran, ignoring thorns. We didn't mind more stings, if they could be healed. Every pore was thirsty.

We tipped our toes in the spring-fed pond. Then our hands. In such a secluded place, we might as well have been in our bathtub. No one could find us. We had tramped this trail a dozen times before without discovering this private cove, the pond just wide enough across for a few lazy strokes.

We were never modest together, our bodies so similar that undressing in front of each other seemed like looking in the mirror. So we lingered. Waited to pull off every last stitch and skinny-dip in the deep. We savored the feel of our sweat-soaked stretchy V-necks that landed right above our navels. Then we peeled the shirts off and did sun salutes in our sports bras. We unzipped our high-tech hiking shorts, then unsuctioned our underthings from our breasts and buttocks, letting them breathe in the breeze. We stretched our necks up to the clouds and said we were works of art.

Art history taught us new vocabulary: The women in paintings were "figures." They weren't naked, they were "nudes." They didn't swim, they "bathed." They had no fur "down there," like children.

We stood in the bubbling froth of the spring and let glistening waves fall over our nipples, mimicking one of our favorite paintings, of the goddess of love riding the water on an oyster. "Look, I'm Venus on the half shell!"

Then we dove in. Our ears filled with water, so we weren't sure we heard anything at first. Footsteps. A small cry of pain: those damn thorns. Someone was watching us.

"Who's there?" we called.

At first all we saw was a rustle of ferns and pokeberry vines. Then someone emerged from the trail we had just tramped down. He had to have been far behind, or we would have heard him before we jumped in. Maybe he had taken a shortcut and hidden in the trees. Maybe he had learned how to disappear in the woods, the way Dad had once taught us. Or maybe we had just not been paying attention.

His breath came quiet, so we figured him an athlete, with lungs so strong he barely had to huff. With arms that long, his fingers stretching out like webs, we guessed he was a swimmer. A star. A fish. He swayed a little, though, off kilter. Must have filled his water bottle with damn strong alcohol.

Then we saw who he was. *That* guy from the life drawing class. Blond hair as yellow as pee. Teeth as white as sin. The guy whose eyes never left us, even to look at the paper in front of him.

"I followed you," he said, crouching at the edge of the water.

"You've been *watching* us?"

"You didn't see me behind the bushes? You put on quite a show. You're like goddesses, you know."

Dad had described us that way all our lives, and it had always scared us.

"Didn't your mom teach you about privacy?" we asked. "Didn't she teach you any manners?"

"You didn't seem to care about that in class."

"Get out!"

But instead he edged closer: khaki shorts and U of M shirt, meticulously scuffed slip-on boat shoes. We thought his kind only moved in packs.

The pond was small. If we left the water, we would give him what he came for: a private viewing of naked women. And God knew he wouldn't stop there. We weren't "figures" in his eyes. Nude bathers? Not to him.

"You can't pretend you don't want it. Not when you go around stripping in public. I don't believe you do it for the paycheck."

"Fuck off." We inhaled all the air, trying to appear bigger and stronger than we were.

He scooped up our clothes and phones. "You come on out, I'll give them back."

How had he missed our rifle? So much stupid inattention. We had been smart enough or lucky enough—or stupid enough ourselves—to drop the pack on the bank opposite where we had shed our clothes. We front-crawled to the other side, then pointed the rifle at him. But before one shot could graze his skin, he fled, as fleet as if we had transformed him into an animal.

Was this why Dad had given us the gun when we turned ten?

Dad had known what we hadn't yet, what we were still learning, that men would always pursue us, then blame us and claim we had been the ones to lure them in.

We argued about the gun more than we fought about anything. We didn't agree whether we should have taken his gift or not, almost half our lifetime ago, if it was an abomination or a necessary evil. The one who had packed the rifle that day asked, "What would you have done without me? Play ukulele to scare that creep away?"

"I never intend to be without you," came the reply.

We emerged from the pond, shaken. We posed like another painting we had seen in art history class, in which the goddess of the hunt turns a spy into a stag, predator into prey. Then we made our way back to campus, shoving every prickly bush and limb clear out of our way.

Many of us sophomores had secrets. We had sworn we would keep ours from everyone except each other, but it became more and more difficult. Our father had killed his father. When our secret leaked out to a few friends, we pretended that killing was a metaphor.

Some of us had other secrets, and it took us twins more than a year or two to wrest these confessions from our classmates:

"I can't stand for anyone to touch me after what happened. Not even to cut my hair."

"I still can't remember how I landed behind a Dumpster in an alley, my hair tangled up with pine needles."

"I stole my mother's pain pills and sold them on the street."

"I have a learning disability."

"I have generalized anxiety disorder and have self-medicated with every household cleaning product in the grocery store."

"My father thinks he is the boss of the world."

"I throw up after every meal."

"I believe in witches, and I think you are one."

"I still wet the bed."

"I have supernatural musical abilities."

"I turned a Peeping Tom into a stag."

"I am the goddess of the hunt."

Our boyfriends shared, too. They said that back in high school Colson had tried to kill himself with pills. Sebastian had helped him learn to meditate and counter dark thoughts with a runner's high. Colson had promised he would never try again, and he and Sebastian had semi-colons inked on their palms, reminding them to "pause but never come to a full stop."

We loved them, of course, even more for their secrets. We never thought, though, that others could love us more for ours.

Some sophomores, we learned, had left behind a little brother who cried until their parents bought him a puppy to replace them. We had left behind a mother who might be eaten up by a lion escaped from the zoo. Or a moose.

We felt guilty for having chosen our life over hers, and we used up a whole box of tissues when we watched movies about mothers and daughters. We hugged at every good-bye, even when our new friends were only driving home for Thanksgiving and we were staying in the dorm with the international students and orphans. We cried at every little thing but not at what we should have. Not when we had left home. We covered our faces with our hands when the Tigers didn't make the playoffs and sobbed when our goldfish went belly-up.

We took the same classes whenever we could, but we were starting to hate it when our professors couldn't tell us apart. We read each other's essays and said, "This is terrible," whenever we thought, *This is better than mine.*

We sometimes crept into bed next to each other at night and lay silent, shining the light of our phones in our eyes, displaying the list of messages from Dad, which we never answered. The subject lines read: "hi," then "call me," then "urgent." They progressed to "where R U?" to "R U dead?" Sometimes they wooed: "I have a present for you." "I forgot to tell you something important." They could be desperate: "PLZ PLZ PLZ." Or "Call!" with an infinity of exclamation points. Finally, simply, "I am your father." Darth Vader's voice echoed off the letters.

We kept expecting him to barge in one day, appear at our door, or even jiggle the lock with a pocketknife and let himself in. He could do anything, we still secretly believed (and even almost hoped, more secretly still). So if he didn't break into our dorm room or our apartment, we figured, his demands to see us must be all bluster.

We deleted the messages, unread. One of us even blocked his number from her phone. The other one yearned to respond when he begged to see us again. Hadn't we punished him enough? He couldn't hurt us anymore. But she told herself: *Next time. Just give my sister time.*

28

In the middle of junior year, we switched beds.

We had seen this plot on sitcoms: *Twins trick boy-friends. Lesson of the episode: Young women, just as you thought, are interchangeable. Dime a dozen? They give them-selves away for free.*

We would prove the cliché wrong. We would change the ending to this: if even identical twins are distinct, think again before you lump all girls together.

We each had our own room in the house we had shared with two other girls since the summer after freshman year. Colson and Sebastian stayed over often. Why not play a little game with them? That night we entered the bath-room together in our sleep clothes—Paula in an oversize band T-shirt long enough to be a minidress and Artis in a cotton camisole and fuzzy Batman bottoms. We emerged, Paula in the cami and fuzz, Artis in the tee—to see if our boyfriends could tell us apart.

We slipped into bed. Wrapped our bellies around our sister's boyfriend's back. Turned off the lights, waited for these boys to notice the slight change in the indent of our hips, the difference in the smells behind our ears, the length of our fingernails, the heat of our breaths. We thought we would last, without detection, five minutes, tops.

Not all night.

Our bedrooms were separated by a thin plaster wall. We listened for thumping from the other side. The sound we had thought was jumping on the bed, when we had heard it from our parents' room, when we were small. Our sister wouldn't go that far, would she, just to prove a point? We had only meant to stay in the game until our boys recognized us for who we were.

But what if we married Sebastian and Colson? We would never know what it was like to be with another boy after him. This might be our only chance.

What if our boyfriends found out? But they wouldn't. Look how clueless they were.

She was probably doing it. Why shouldn't we? We didn't want to know about it, though.

We heard animal noises through our window screens, but maybe it was the sound of skunks in heat or toms on the prowl. We heard moaning, which sounded like dreaming. We felt something, too. A current. A cupping palm, a thrusting hip, a wandering fingertip. Maybe just a reverie, the imagined pleasure of the other. We turned over on our sides and opened wide, careful not to squeak the springs.

We were as bad as Dad, weren't we? *My God.* Cheating

was too easy. We hadn't meant to. Maybe he hadn't, either.

Our boys traced their fingers over the birthmarks and scars we didn't share. They cupped our bellies, one sinewy, the other supple. But they didn't say they could tell the difference. They didn't say a thing. The trick was on us.

Our eyes wouldn't close. The night was like day, but we stayed still anyway, careful not to wake the house. Good was like bad. Fast was like slow. We wanted to do it again, but we also wanted to bust our own butts. We lay in the beds we had made for ourselves, only half understanding what we had just done.

Maybe we had really switched, as we had back when we were little and thought we were witches. Maybe we were, then and now.

The next morning, as always, we ran before dawn. The boys woke when we returned, our tiny clingy shorts damp with sweat.

"How did you sleep?" they asked.

We hadn't slept. Keeping our bodies apart from theirs on such narrow beds required too much care, hour after hour, through a night as dark as the dark side we hadn't known we had.

But we couldn't tell them that, so we turned our heads. Not away from our boys, but from each other. We kept turning, too, every day, this new distance invisible to anyone but us.

Were they really that unaware? Had they sleepwalked through sex? Or pretended to be fooled, enjoying the temporary trade? We would never know. No way we would ever ask.

We divvied up our skirts and shirts. Mine. Yours. No more common drawers.

At breakfast, we plugged in earbuds and ignored each other. The wind chilled. Ice cream would not have melted, had we held it in our laps for days. The wind groaned through the cracks around the front door.

We played a regular gig at the Crypt, an open mic in the basement of St. Paul's Chapel on campus, Paula's mermaid voice floating over her riffs on guitar or violin, Artis the muscle of rhythm on electric bass or cello, sometimes forgetting to plug in, though no one ever noticed if she did. No one would have noticed if she hadn't shown up at all, but we both pretended we didn't know that.

We returned from runs only as the dark evaporated into pink on the horizon. One of us wanted to join track, but the other said we didn't have time if we wanted to keep writing songs. Wasn't running every morning enough? Or too much.

"You don't have to go with me."

"It's safer with two." We both knew one was the scariest number.

We couldn't agree on one focus, so we double-majored in music and environmental science. Outside class, we were either practicing with our band, with the string quartet led by Mr. Hadadd's old professor, or plugging numbers into a database for our work-study job for a meteorology professor.

The numbers were grim. "In ten years," our professor said, "the planet could reach a crucial threshold, causing drought, wildfires, and floods. Blizzards and hurricanes, tsunamis and earthquakes could all become as commonplace as summer thundershowers. We're two-thirds of the way there."

Ten years was half our entire lives. The time stretched out long in front of us, like an early morning shadow. Our boyfriends said we should change the name of our band to Weather Women.

Staver met Mom and Ya-Ya many times. Their family lived in the Metro area, too, so it was easy to hitch a ride home with them. We always chose a day Dad would be away on a hunting trip. The logistics were easy. He was gone more and more. Ya-Ya was sick, so we visited her whenever we could. Not just her body but her brain had slowed, which is why Staver wasn't offended when she didn't address them as "them."

"That's not the right word," she said. "I don't speak perfect, but I have good enough English to know that."

Ya-Ya complimented Staver's dresses as much as their ties and tucked-in shirts. Sometimes she got confused by the attire and thought they were two different people. That made Staver sway their hips and puff out their flat chest. "Two *at least*."

No wonder we could sit in easy silence on those road trips together. No need to explain our own odd equations.

On Christmas break, our boys met our girls—first Mom, then Ya-Ya. As soon as we walked in, Mom handed us babies and asked us to spoon mashed overripe bananas and pulverized rice into their gummy mouths. Our boys were better at care and feeding than we were, which should have made us proud, but it scared us instead. Because we worried that our mother-parts were defective? Because we wondered if our sweethearts were really boys after all? Even years later, we still couldn't put that shuddery jolt into words.

"Good workers," Mom said as we left. Her highest praise. We were back in the car before we realized she'd been giving them a test.

"A package deal," Ya-Ya said, when she first met them. "Just like you two."

We cringed to hear her say those words, so unromantic, so transactional. And yet. She was still sharp.

In our boys' shared car, we drove to their hometown, halfway between Up North and Down State, two hours up from the city. It was spring break, the cherry blossoms not yet in bloom, and dark, short days lingering like phlegm that can't be cleared from the throat. Every year longer winters, weirder weather.

We met Colson's parents for lunch, Sebastian's for dinner. Colson's father, a cardiologist with big ears, invited us to stay in his country house some summer. In Martha's Vineyard. "Isn't that expensive?" we said, and the parents laughed. We stared at our scuffed boots, thrift store beaded sweaters pilling under the arms, and socks woven with pictures of pizza slices with wings.

Colson and Sebastian wore khakis and polos when they visited their parents, leaving their usual black clothes and skinny jeans, their piercings and hair gel and snarky T-shirts out of their parents' view. It had never occurred to us that it was possible to show a different side to your parents than you showed to everyone else, to reserve a private part of yourself they couldn't mess with.

Colson's mother, a high school English teacher with a radio voice, asked if we could read each other's minds. We waited for the sly smile to creep up her face, telling us she was joking, of course, and there it was. People always were joking when they asked this question.

We didn't tell her that when we were little, we said we could do mind tricks. That we could predict what card our sister picked but that we hadn't tried it since then. We had been too good at it. The only witches people want to hear about are the ones in children's books, the ones we all love to hate.

She asked if Colson had met our family. We told her both our boyfriends had met our mom.

"And your dad?"

"He's always out of town when we come home." We didn't have to say we planned it that way.

We had been eating with them more and more. Fancy meals like we had never had at home. Truffle deviled duck eggs. Brick oven pizza with goat cheese and capers. Their houses had names, like "colonial" or "split-level." They had separate rooms for playing piano and watching TV. They never stormed around or banged cymbals in the basement. They called the basement "the rec room." They folded their napkins into swans and kept the music low enough to talk over. "We want to adopt your parents," we told Colson and Sebastian after one of our meals.

"You don't know them," they said. "I bet we'd think your dad's cool, if you'd let us meet him."

"You want to?"

"Of course," they both said at exactly the same time.

"Jinx! Pinky links!" We took a hand from each and entwined the little fingers.

They didn't squirm at each other's touch. They grabbed each other's hands and squeezed, in public, boy to boy. That made us love them even more.

What could Dad do to us in front of our boyfriends? We could always leave the house and jump into the car.

So we planned a reunion. A homecoming. If home meant not where you came from but who. We would bring our boys for dinner, just one meal, we said. No other contact. Mom found a weekend when Dad would be home. "Not easy as peas," Ya-Ya said.

One of us packed a present for Dad, without telling the other she had. A CD she knew he would groove to. She had also written him a song she planned to sing to him in person. She kept staring at herself in the mirror, practicing a soft gaze, a tender smile. The other just tried to forget she had agreed to such a stupid thing.

That Saturday we drove with our boyfriends to the city early enough to take Ya-Ya to the Greek festival first. Every week was a different country's cuisine on the Detroit River. They called it the Ethnic Festival, which now sounded like something we would study in an anthropology class.

We wore band T-shirts, neon Converse, and headbands holding up messy buns. We drew cat eyes but left our lips bare. Colson and Sebastian wore tight ironic T-shirts we had picked out for them and black thumbnails they had let us paint. We slurped flaming cheese drizzled with lemon. Scooped up orzo with feta and olives. Tore into lamb with rosemary and mint. A bearded man in a cloak paced the length of the river, shouting out the Greek alphabet. He looked like the same one we had seen on campus the day Mr. Haddad had taken us for a tour. We thought, for the first time, that maybe Detroit wasn't so different from Ann Arbor.

Then we saw Dad. He was smaller than we remembered. Thinner maybe, but not exactly physically. Off kilter, assuming he'd ever been on. But unmistakably him, the fire still sizzling at his fingertips. What we noticed most, though, was the way he was standing with his arms around the bare shoulders of a woman much plumper than Mom. We could see only enough to tell that her hair gleamed with diamond light.

Ya-Ya didn't see them, and we whisked her away before she did. We didn't want her to make a scene like she had that time at the shoe department at Penney's.

He wasn't supposed to be back in the city yet, we said to each other with our jutting chins. Mom had said he'd be out hunting until dinnertime. Hunting what, she hadn't said.

After we dropped Ya-Ya back at her house, we went home to tell Mom what we had seen. Let the first time our boyfriends met Dad be the day that Mom left him.

But she didn't. Instead, she swirled a spoon in her coffee and said, "Of course women love him."

We dropped our own spoons at the same time. Our boyfriends chewed their lips.

"That's all you have to say?" we demanded. "It's always the woman's fault?"

"He's not an ordinary man. And he gives me what I need."

Here we had to stop her. We didn't want to know any more about our parents' sex lives. We knew too much already, having grown up in this small house with thin walls.

Dad was not too big to fall. Like some kind of god.

We'd show him.

We changed our plans and piled into the car. Dad could wait. Let him stew. Let him guess we had found him out and decided to punish him. Somebody needed to. We blasted the music, bass amped to ten, and fled.

29

*I*n psychology class, our professor stood in front of the large classroom in a shift printed with bold geometric shapes and lectured on delusions. She had an Eastern European accent we couldn't place, which she seemed to compensate for by shouting into the microphone. Some of us have delusions of control—she said, and we wrote—like the belief that our thoughts can be heard by others, the belief that others are inserting thoughts into our heads, or the belief that people are stealing thoughts from our brains.

Some of us believe we are already dead. This is called Cotard delusion.

Some of us become stalkers, convinced a celebrity is in love with us.

Some of us believe different people are all just a single person who changes shape. This delusion is associated with brain lesions or damage.

Some of us believe we are immortal. Up to half of us with Cotard delusion believe we can't die.

Some of us have delusions of jealousy and collect "evidence" of nonexistent infidelities.

Some of us have delusions of persecution. We may believe the government is tapping our phone lines, that we have been wrongfully identified as a terrorist, or attacked, cheated, conspired against, followed, harassed, obstructed, poisoned, or spied upon.

Some of us have religious delusions. Though shared beliefs considered normal for a particular religion or culture are not regarded as delusions.

Some of us believe that random events have significant meaning. This is called a delusion of reference.

Some of us believe we are a deity, or that we have special powers, rare abilities, or hidden talents. This is called delusions of grandeur. (*Some of us name our twins after Apollo and Artemis.*)

Some of us believe another person can read our minds. (*Did we say that aloud to each other or just think it?*)

Some of us had delusions? How about all?

The professor didn't really say "some of us." She said "some patients." But we always implicated ourselves. Maybe that's a mental illness, too, the "delusion of inclusion."

Some of us were deluded. Some in this classroom, most likely. Not only some of *them.* Some of *us.*

Maybe it was a question of degree. Some of us had it bad.

Like Dad.

Heroes and Monsters was our favorite class, the stories as familiar as the hair on our necks. Heroes and Monsters was also our least favorite class, for the same reason. The day the professor lectured on Zeus, we squeezed the bunched strands of our hair so tight in their elastic bands our heads hurt.

Maybe it was fated that we would take this class and psychology and piece together Dad's condition. His fiction. His alternate reality. Those of us who believed in fate suffered from a delusion of reference. Hadn't our professor just said that?

Maybe we chose these classes because we needed someone to point out the obvious. Maybe we already knew more than we would admit.

We hid in our hoodies. We wore them backward in our rooms, erasing our faces. When we took the hoods off, the patterns from the cotton left mottles on our sensitive skin.

We texted Mom. We imagined her carrying the babies while she typed on her phone, their spit-up drooling down the screen, their tantrums bubbling up over knocked-down blocks. We sat on the library steps in the sun while Colson and Sebastian played Frisbee with Staver and a guy from chemistry lab.

"Does Dad have delusions of grandeur?" we asked her.

"I don't know what you're talking about," came her swift reply.

"Did you take him to the doctor?"

"You know your Dad. He doesn't believe in doctors. Why?"

"He thinks he's some kind of god," we said.

"You don't think he is?"

We had never known Mom had a sense of humor. She had to be joking, though she didn't use the right emojis to say so.

We remembered the stories Ya-Ya used to tell to distract us on boring walks or rides in the car. Stories from the Old Country: Jason capturing the Golden Fleece, Theseus slaying the Minotaur, Daedalus flying on his feathery wings. As children, we had believed in them as much as we had believed in Santa Claus and unicorns. Maybe Mom still did.

We talked on Snapchat so our words would evaporate. So Dad wouldn't see and think we were out to get him. He might also have delusions of persecution.

Then we asked the question we had asked ourselves for years. The kind of question we didn't want to ask in email or in person, either. We would tremble too much, and our voices would fray. This way, all traces of conversation would disappear as soon as they were read.

We typed, "Did Dad kill Papu?"

Nothing but a blank screen in response. We didn't hear back from her at all for a long, long time.

Which we took as a bad sign.

We finally told Sebastian and Colson about Dad and Papu, about death and delusions. Zeus killed Cronus, his dad, we said. So if Dad thought he was Zeus, he might have thought he had to kill his dad. That it was even the heroic thing to do.

This was our definition of intimacy: trusting people enough to tell them our secrets. This was our true loss of virginity: telling the first time. All those high school hookups were nothing in comparison. We had not been ready to reveal anything yet. Even to ourselves.

We wanted to change our names to reflect what we now knew, but we just changed the name of our band.

Now we were the Twin Delusions. We pressed our heads into our hands, then our fingernails—all twenty sharp claws—into our tender knees.

30

Colson and Sebastian had the car. Sebastian had the conveniently located friend. "Bring sleeping bags," the friend said. Staver came along for the ride, making us five.

We had always wanted to crash on someone's floor for spring break. We had always wanted to visit New York City, though we had never left Michigan.

None of us knew how to parallel park, so we left the car at a friend's parents' house in Queens and took the train to Sebastian's friend's place in Sunset Park, the Chinatown of Brooklyn. It was a closetless fourth-floor walk-up over a bowling alley. A clanky pot rack dominated the kitchen, a keyboard and drum set the living room. The heat blasted so high we had to open the windows, letting in squeaking and singing: rice pots, mattress springs, and lullabies in other languages.

We wore thick boots and army surplus down, even though the sidewalks here no longer slogged with slush, as in Ann Arbor. The air was warm enough to smell the trash, rotting fish heads and a fecund trace of bean paste.

We—girls, boyfriends, and Staver—took the R train

and got off at Ninth Street and Fourth Avenue in Brooklyn. We flashed our new IDs in tiny music clubs, drinking milky-bottled beer and listening to a chorus of accordions.

We retrieved the car and drove to a club in Fort Greene almost smaller than the elfin apartment we stayed in. We looked so long for a parking spot, we almost missed the first act.

We took the R train and changed to the L train to Williamsburg. We drank black ale and heard bagpipes, electric cellos, and miniature marching bands.

We took the train the other way, to Coney Island. We dipped our toes in the ocean, for the first time. We looked out into the blue, and we spotted Greece. Almost. We sucked mangoes on sticks hawked by vendors on bicycles and listened for the bats to crack at the far end of the beach, but it wasn't baseball season yet.

Finally we ventured into Manhattan, arriving hours early to add our name to the list for open mic night at the Catacombs. Sebastian's friend assured us that this dark basement space on the edge of the West Side Highway was the "it" club for live music. We wore one of our girl-band costumes, a hodgepodge of thrift shop mismatch. Ruby slippers, silver sequined tank tops, skinny black cigarette pants. Hair in high slicked-back ponytails, Super Girl–style. Lipstick as red as our shoes, applied a minute before we performed and wiped off a minute after.

Tables filled. We scarfed the still-warm tamales we had

smuggled inside in our pockets from the bodega near where we were staying.

We swallowed the idea that our talent was a delusion. We were Paula and Artis. *Not* Apollo and Artemis, no matter how much Dad pretended. Maybe our YouTube fame had all been in our heads.

We had signed up so early we were the first to play. Alone on the stage, we breathed in the room.

"Marco," we whispered, so soft no one could have heard us.

"Polo" came the reply, perhaps a thought or a nod.

We tapped on thighs. Tapped again. Twisted the single diamond earring we each wore.

Then came guitar, electric bass, and voice. Song gushed out like water from a hose. Strong long lines. Trembling vibrato. The liquid melodies haunted us, as if we weren't the ones playing them.

All talking hushed. All clinking of glasses and shuffling of feet. Beer bottles hovered in midair, between tables and mouths. Servers sat. First dates dropped their poses. Friends forgot the punchline to their in-jokes. Couples leaned on tables, their forearms in sphinx pose.

We stopped time. We could have led them back to ancient Greece if we had wanted to.

We sang about first blood between our legs. About cheating to lose the spelling bee. About falling in love with a gun and hating ourselves for it. We sang about pixies and trying on shoes. Getting lost in the woods. Bathing nude and pointing a gun at a peeping boy with yellow hair. A gun that turned him into the animal he really was. Changing ourselves into weapons. And back.

We were children again. We were children of gods. We had never heard of delusions. We were full of belief. We were fresh. We forgot. We were lost. We tripped and flipped and wriggled our hips and were back in our garage at our fifteenth birthday party when the thunder boomed as our rhythm section, the sky our backup band.

Were we deluded? Maybe. But our delusion was so potent the whole club was in on it. Or part of it. We felt like gods. Maybe we were. Who knew? Maybe not our psychology professor.

After we floated back to our seats for the break between acts, a man twice our age, wiry and small, with double-pierced ears and a scarf around his neck, scooted his chair between us at our table. His thumbs were as callused as ours. On second look, we saw that his scarf concealed a dark tattoo against his pink skin. Of what, we couldn't tell. He asked, "Are you the Slutty Twins?"

Sebastian and Colson raised their fists, but we clamped them down. They didn't know who we were. Who we had been.

We said nothing. We had been followed back then. We had been stalked. That name was trouble.

"I'm a fan," the man said. He opened his mouth, and

we smelled milk stout. Never a good combination. "I watched your videos a hundred times. But then they disappeared. What happened?"

"What's it to you?" our boyfriends asked. They leaned into us, becoming human shields.

"I'm a record producer," he said. "Name's Django. I always come for talent night, but I never score this big."

"Nobody's scoring with anybody," Sebastian said.

"Get your hand off her knee," Colson told Django. But his hands dug deep into his pockets.

"Can I buy you a drink?" Django asked.

Still no answer.

"Can I buy you dinner? I've heard enough, let's get out of here."

His eyes never left Paula. But he wasn't peering down her shirt. He wasn't acting like men his age often did. He was looking at her throat, mesmerized by her instrument.

Django took us to a nearby restaurant. We all insisted Colson and Sebastian and Staver had to come. We didn't know this man, and he promised too much to be for real.

But he was. For Paula, at least. "I only want the singer," he said, after paying the check.

We couldn't have foreseen he would say that, could we? As soon as he did, though, it was like déjà vu. We had imagined this moment. We had always known that someone would try to separate us. We intertwined our fingers. We didn't mean to squeeze so hard our rings bore holes in our skin. But we didn't mind hurting each other. All that mattered, at the moment, was feeling the same thing.

One of us switched her heels for the flats in her bag. One of us threw on a sweater. One of us pulled out the rubber band and let her hair waterfall over her eyes. The other one didn't.

At graduation, when we were twenty-two, we opened the time capsule that held the letter we had written to our future selves when we were twelve.

In that letter we had predicted we would always live in the same town, play in the same band. One of us would never win if that meant the other had to lose. We would never compete twin against twin, and this pact would guarantee that we would never have to part. If one was about to win, the other would *try* to lose. No question: two for one, or none for none, the only choices. Dad hadn't known how right we were to "cheat" at the spelling bee, but we knew how wrong he had been. Or thought we did.

Because Django had said, "I only want the singer," and only one of us could really sing.

The letter in our twelve-year-old loopy handwriting read, "All we know now is that we'll always be together." The one thing we thought we knew, back then, was *wrong*.

31

We remembered little from the years we lived apart, from twenty-three to twenty-nine.

How could we live, apart? We could and we couldn't. We did. And we didn't.

All we recall are a few scattered events. They're thin and faint, like music streamed from a single earbud.

After college, we tried to email or text every day. "You alive?" or "Good night." At least that. So we lived those years together, even when our jobs flung us all over the world. Whatever happened to one of us seemed to happen to the other. Whenever one of us touched her single diamond stud, the other touched its mate.

When Artis entered Army Ranger training, with Sebastian, in southern Georgia, both of us twins sweated in our swampy boots. When Paula moved into the same Sunset Park walk-up over a bowling alley where we had crashed for spring break, when she played dim-lit clubs and waited dim sum tables while Colson enrolled at Teacher's College, both of us could smell the bean paste and hear the jangle of woks from Brooklyn Chinatown. When Artis learned computer code to control drones, both of us felt our fingers cramp from so much tapping at the keyboard. When Paula pierced her nose and inked her arm, we both could feel the flesh sting.

When one of us cut her hair (military rules), the other did, too, the same day. (Easier to spike and add neon color that way.)

"Hey Artis," Paula wrote. "Send me a whole body selfie. If I use it for my album cover, people will think I'm ripped. I'm going for the waif look. Either that or I'm an actual starving artist."

"Hey Paula," Artis wrote. "Shipping out soon. Good news is spousal death benefits for Rangers are phenomenal. Wouldn't want mine to go to waste. How about you and Colson make it a double wedding? XO, Artis"

We had never imagined getting married any other way.

We eloped, if you can use such a sexy word for a military-dress wedding at an army base, flanked by recent Ranger graduates, plus Staver and their partner, in a bright suit and cowboy boots, an antidote to the sober uniforms some other guests wore. No time for a regular ceremony before entering the combat zone, we told our families and imminent in-laws. We didn't say we wanted to keep Dad away.

We flew Mom out to Martha's Vineyard that summer. She stayed with us in Colson's family's summer house, closing her daycare for a week. Whenever she mentioned

Dad, we turned away. We took the cards he had asked her to pass on to us and tossed them in the trash.

Our friends asked us why we had married so young. We didn't say what we knew. That living without a twin was waking up each morning with only one arm, one leg, one eye, one ear, one thought: More. Give us more. We told each other: If I can't live with you, a husband will have to do.

We wore our single diamond studs to the wedding. We were girly and not. Simple and fancy. Half and half. The hole in one earlobe empty, the other full.

We changed. We (Artis and Sebastian) deployed to Afghanistan. Pakistan. Environmental science experts, predicting the effects of weather on land mines. We had close calls. We both lost friends. Others lost legs or arm or eyes. One friend OD'd on the way to a gig. We lost track.

We (Paula and the band; Colson in the audience) played in coffee shops and storefront bars, in galleries and at festivals. At house parties and in church basements. We collected fives and tens from the hat passed around to pay our electricity bill so we could continue to play our amped-up violin. We released an album, *Weather Woman*, and hoped for just a little bit of fame, nothing viral like the Slutty Twins. We glanced over our shoulders for stalking lechers or amphetamined paparazzi. Django, our manager, said, "You're too young to always be looking back."

The Rangers were sent on a peacekeeping mission to Palestine. As if there were peace to keep. Next year, they said, we'll send drones instead.

Robots could drive and fold clothes, but they couldn't yet make art. The video for the single "Weather Woman" became a meme. That didn't translate into royalties.

We thought being married meant we would never have to be lonely. Our husbands cooked us roasted eggplant with smoked mozzarella over fettucine, scrubbed pots and cupped our bellies and massaged our soles. And yet.

We wondered if adopting a dog would help. Or having an affair.

Maybe if we had more fans. More sales. A higher rank. More gun power. We ate dinner, our husbands scooping chili and rice into their mouths across the table from us, smiling and clinking their beer bottles against ours. We smiled back, but inside, we crumpled into our bowls. We didn't tell our men what was wrong. It was nothing they could fix. Hadn't we warned them they were marrying only half a bride?

We wanted more. More feet. More hands. More mouths to feed. More cells. More us. We patted the concave gap in our bellies, then felt it, month by month, fill up.

Hey A,

I wrote you a song about your pregnancy. It's called Expecting and it starts like this:

You are swaying to the rhythm of bread rising
Buoyant with waiting
Trickling into the ocean with your big toe
Panting with foamy breath from so much carrying
Then swoosh! You float—
The icing of expectation holds you up

XO

A: I knew it! You're pregnant, too.
P: I'm not even showing yet.
A: You forgot I can read your mind.

We gave birth. Two brown boys, one lighter than the other. Barack and Pablo. One of them looked just like his grandfather the cardiologist, all ears and fuzzy head. The other Sebastian's double. Both with rounded faces and chins. Would we have to admit that it was true, as the ancient Greeks proposed, that babies only inherited from their fathers?

A fault line from Portland to Seattle caused the biggest

earthquake in recent history. Sea levels rose, and coastal houses, once worth millions, couldn't be sold for scraps. We wondered what we could have done if we hadn't become singer and soldier, leading the lives Dad trained us for. We might have changed the world. Or was that a delusion of grandeur?

One of us took a three-month maternity leave, back in the States. Then Sebastian took paternity leave.

One of us started writing songs about birth. Who knew there was such a big market for music about motherhood? Colson got a job teaching in the Bronx, finally allowing the move to an apartment with hot water.

One of us wanted her baby to meet his maternal grandfather. One of us said, "If you visit him, you're dead to me." Guess which twin won that argument? The one who knew how to give orders.

A: I bought a copy of your album for Mom.

P: That explains the one sale we had this month.

A: Ha ha. She liked it.

P: I bet she enjoyed my descriptions of our crappy childhood.

A: Come on. It wasn't that bad.

Pause for comic effect.

A: The *album*, I mean.

On the subway or in a chopper, a flash through our bodies, a zap. We each knew when something happened to our sister. She twisted her wrist leading training exercises with new recruits. Or she tripped on stage. Broke a leg or a heart or a record. We knew when she healed, too. We saw calm wash over the sky, a denim prewash dye.

A: Somebody stole my guns. Just now while we were out to dinner.
P: They steal your diamond stud?
A: I never take it off.
P: I'd know if you did.
A: Wish I'd been home.
P: So you could shoot the guy?
A: So I could protect my family. I worry about yours.
P: Maybe I should buy a gun.
A: Exactly.
P: So somebody could break in and steal it.

One of us played at Madison Square Garden, sandwiched between the circus and a basketball game. How had the band gotten so big?

We had changed diapers and nursed at two-hour

intervals and given up coffee and gluten and dairy to try to stop colic, and we were so bleary-eyed we looked like vampires. Then we woke up one day (had we even slept?), and we were filling auditoriums and writing code for an army of drones that could reduce American military casualties by half.

We spent holidays with our in-laws, still meeting Mom only when we knew Dad was away. We flew in for Ya-Ya's funeral but left the same day and in the crush of relatives managed not to talk to Dad at all. When Mom mentioned his name, we pretended we didn't hear.

We befriended rock stars and heroes. We didn't know what those words meant, but they sounded good. Some people used them to describe us.

We shook our fingertips, and the sky expanded with storm, just like Dad had taught us, though we never admitted he had. We flicked our wrists and lightning flickered. We harnessed this power into our guitars and guns.

Some days we almost forgot we had a family, besides each other and our doting husbands, sons, and dogs. Then one day, we were forced to remember.

Part Three

32

*I*t started with the call that came the same time every year: "Come home." We could almost hear Mom lean into the palm that held her cell, almost see her other hand twisting a ringlet that had fallen from her bun, legs jiggling with enough nervous energy to light a window display. "Please come see your family for Christmas."

We wanted to make her happy. But we didn't want to see Dad.

So we said, "Not this time. Maybe next year." Our throats burned with the rawness of our lies.

Mom told our sons that Michigan was the land of perpetual snow, so they begged us to take them there. She didn't admit that these snowstorms were monstrous. Ten years had passed since our meteorology professor said they would be. Not every place had warmed. In Michigan the weather just became weirder.

"The state is even shaped like a giant mitten," Mom said. The boys spun around and around, littering the floor with shredded paper, shouting, "White Christmas!"

Then we texted each other:

"Wish we could take the boys to Michigan."

We could if Dad was gone.

The words were too terrible to say aloud or to tap out on our phones, but we couldn't stop the thought from creeping in. That we wanted him out of the way. Not hunting. Not working. But gone for good.

We had barely finished texting when Mom rang again. The summoning call came in the dark, a slit of moon lighting our phones.

"Dad," she said.

We almost knew what would come next. No, we *did* know.

"Dead."

Decades removed and several states away, we could still hear each other's twin cries. A common foe had fallen. A foe who had kept us connected.

As soon as we hung up with Mom, we called each other. We tapped our thighs, clicked our tongues, whistled air through sore throats. One of us started a tune the other finished. Our wordless words said:

"We did this to him."

"You heard what Mom said. Cardiac arrest."

"That could be a symptom, not a cause."

"I didn't know he had a heart to be attacked."

"Marco," one of us finally said aloud.

"Polo," the other replied. Then our voices ground down to hums.

Mom couldn't have said what we thought she had. Not because Dad was too young. People die young every day. But because he was sturdier than the rest of us. Because he learned in the army how to survive. Because he could hack Alaska. Because his skin was like tree bark. Because we were too young to be fatherless. Because our children had not yet met him. Because we didn't understand our power. Because he was . . .

What was the word we had learned in fourth grade? The word that had told us we had infinite time to change our minds. *Immortal.* We believed in this word, whether we realized it or not, till we couldn't anymore.

We didn't remember saying good-bye on the phone. We didn't think we had hung up. But in the morning our husbands found us still on the floor, flopped there like fish. We downed coffee strong as whiskey, bought tickets, and packed our bags. Then, at last, we flew.

33

We returned to our parents' house, parents ourselves. It had been how many years since we came home for Christmas, the trips endlessly "postponed"? Our new homes were hundreds of miles and hundreds of dollars away, and we had said we were too busy changing diapers and changing our names.

At the funeral, the priest spoke partly in Greek, and we didn't understand. In English, he said Dad was in heaven.

Dad's friends said, in their eulogies, "He's not gone, he's just merged with the eternal." They said, "He returned to a better place." "He's in the mind of God." "He's up in the sky looking down." "He's waiting for us to join him in the clouds."

Looking down on *us*, for sure.

Who knew Dad had had so many friends? So many came, even though the horrible weather encouraged hunkering down at home. More than one person said, "He always shoveled my walk"; someone else said, "That man could charm the teeth out of a lion's mouth"; someone else, "There aren't many like him left." Had we accidentally crashed the wrong funeral?

Wild Pete, Dad's sidekick in Alaska, limped up to the podium. "The sky opened up today, and one of their own returned home."

Everyone stared at us. Especially one man. His purple skinny tie was as pointy as his fuzzy chin.

After the funeral, we stood next to the coffin with Mom and greeted all the people Dad hadn't managed to piss off enough his whole life to alienate. More than we had ever seen at a funeral for someone who wasn't famous. Men he had worked with at Ford. Guys he had played cards with at the VFW. Neighbors, tow truck customers. Even some army buddies. People said, "He wasn't like the rest of us. That's the best way I can describe him."

Ms. Rosen, still wearing her signature long skirts and dangly bracelets, squeezed us in a hug and kissed the tops of our heads, as if we still only came up to her armpits. She recounted the time Dad had trained our class for the spelling bee. He had returned every year to coach, she said.

"We didn't know," we said.

You didn't know squat. Did she say that aloud or just burn it into us with her eyes?

Next in line was the man with the purple tie who had glared at us across the aisle. He pulled tissues from his pants and offered them, but we shook our heads. Was he mocking our dry eyes with his, puffed red? Then he plucked two business cards from the other pocket and planted them in our palms. He was a software designer for human prosthetics. Ezekiel. "Call me Zeke," was the first thing he said. "It's what my family calls me."

Wild Pete was next in the receiving line. He clawed us raw with his weathered skin. Mouth lost in beard, swaying arms furry with gray. He smelled like mulch and wet chewing tobacco. "So you're the girls who killed your old man?"

"How could you say that?" we said to him. To each other, only with our eyes, we replied, *How did he know?*

We slid away, through the back door, into the storm. Wild Pete muttered to the others as we left. All we heard was, *Huff huff huff.* Then *Those damn girls.*

You killed your dad. We had heard it before. That's what Ya-Ya had said to Dad at his own father's funeral.

Hadn't we left so we wouldn't become like him? But look: we had.

We propped ourselves against brick. We toppled onto each other, elbow to elbow, hip to hip.

"Wild Pete's right. We killed him," we said into empty air.

"Not too loud." But there was no one to hear. Everyone else lingered in the church, though the funeral had ended ages ago. Soon they would find us out here, if the snow didn't bury us or render us invisible.

"We caused a heart attack with our thoughts? That's not the kind of world we live in." We said this as the sky fell onto the middle of the country and the sea rose up and swallowed the edges of land. As the fires swooped down in the west like a dragon disturbed in its lair. What kind of world did we live in again?

"We've made things happen with our minds before."

In a flash we saw ourselves on Groundhog Day so long ago, when we had said, "Make it spring," and the mounds of snow melted into mush. In the truck when Dad had taught Mom to drive. We had thought the word *stop* and made the truck stand still.

"No one would believe us."

"No one would believe we talk to each other like this, either," we silently said. "Tell the army you're hearing voices, and you'll be put on disability. If you're lucky they'll call it a casualty of PTSD."

This thing, this thing we could do, this thing we had done to Dad, we hated this thing, even if it was what had turned us into singers and soldiers, rock stars and heroes. The ability to want something so much we made it so. We didn't know what this thing was, but we knew where it had come from.

Him.

We hung onto each other's fingers. Our only hope to stay up, we knew, was to find a way to hold each other.

We seemed to stay there for years.

We watched the rerun of our lives from the time of Papu's funeral to Dad's. We might have remained in the

cold till our own last rites if our husbands hadn't excavated us and defrosted our fingers with the heat behind
their necks.

Colson and Sebastian had somehow wrangled our sons
and our mom, wrapped the leftovers in plastic, loaded the
cars, then driven home to our parents' house. Mom's house.
That new phrase sounded so small.

34

*W*e tucked in our sons, warm on the floor next to the beds we would share with their dads. Mom popped a pill and collapsed even before the boys did. She had relinquished her room for the couch. She couldn't bear a half-empty bed, she said, and watched TV until her eyelids closed and the living room became a sea of snores.

We drank while the rest of the house slept. We listened to our men, their deep breathing synchronized and loud in the small house. We listened to our little boys.

Our elbows on the Formica kitchen table, moon shining on snow through gauzy curtains our only light, we guzzled the Jack Daniels Dad used to spoon-feed us. Medicine to make us tough. We took turns from the same glass, and now it made us soft instead. We could have cut each other with butter knives.

One of us said we should have visited for Christmas. At least once in a while. At least *once.* We didn't have to stay away just because he had grounded us all those years ago. Because he had threatened to have our tubes tied, to sterilize us like animals. We didn't need to cut him off just because he had killed his dad.

The other said it was all his fault, the prick. What about our bruises?

But maybe everyone had them, back in the days of corporal punishment. It took two to fight. Or three.

We had always fought with him about the heat, so now we turned it up high. Not that we would ever let our own children play with the thermostat.

Dad would have loved the snow-glow through the window. This was his favorite season, frozen mounds turning white to gray to charcoal, the drifts so deep bodies could be buried in them and not discovered until the Easter thaw. Dad had worn a winter beard, his fur, without a coat. "It's better to be too cold than too hot," he said. "You can always put more on in the winter. But in the summer there's only so much you can take off.

"Remember his Christmas lights?" we said, lacing our hands, prayerlike, on the table. We nodded and he appeared, sprung from the sharp edges of our knuckles.

He had yelled, "Kids! You'll never guess what I brought home." But we could. It was always the same. Colored lights and white lights. Icicle lights and blinking lights. Lights that spelled Merry Christmas and motion-detection lights that played his favorite Christmas song: "You better watch out, you better not cry, you better not pout, I'm telling you why." The boxes blurred and became bottomless, an endless loop of lights.

"Know why Christmas is in winter?" he had asked.

"Because of solstice?" we had said. Our third-grade science unit was on the sun and moon.

"Solstice is for pagans," Dad had said. "Winter is dark; Christmas has lights."

The colder the air, the happier Dad was, showing off for Mrs. Tuck next door. We watched her watch him through her picture window as he shoveled snow in only a muscle shirt, his biceps glistening.

We stopped hoping the boxes he brought home would be presents for us: pogo sticks or friendship bracelet kits. They were always lights.

We complained to each other but bragged to the neighbors. Dad was Santa Claus, we told them, our whole block the North Pole. Lots of kids had pogo sticks, we said, but whose house lit up the whole Milky Way? After the electricity was cut, the lights bill too high, the icicles and candles hung dark, sadder than no decorations at all. Dad refused to take them down. And he kept buying them, the surplus strings filling up the garage. What a gyp, we had said, only to each other, the zombie lights mocking us almost as much as the neighbor kids did.

We hadn't even gotten presents that year. Had we?

From the backyard Dad's latest hound howled at the moon, after midnight already. He wasn't Dad's anymore. Who did any of us belong to now?

We thought we'd always belong to each other. As surely as one season turns to the next. Yet outside the window, moonlight turning snow into falling stars, this hungry winter just might rage forever. And look at us, averting our eyes like strangers on the subway.

What could we count on anymore?

Not *you*.

With that singular word, the cold came inside.

35

*W*e're no better than dogs, running away." We weren't the ones who spoke this time. It was just me, Paula, pounding my fist on the table.

My puny biceps didn't do much damage. Artis could have knocked a hole right through.

I downed the dregs of whiskey, the alcohol singeing my throat. It hurt like burning off a wart and made my voice melt when I said, "He took care of all of us the year the lights went out. Remember?"

"I'd rather not," Artis snarled at me. We had argued plenty with him, through the years, but never *about* him before.

"*Don't* be a coward." Maybe the whiskey made me use Dad's words, with his emphasis, which always implied "or I'll make you regret it."

My sister faced the window, hot breath on frost, pretending she hadn't heard me. I told her how the night the lights died was Christmas Eve. Dad had excavated camping gear, and we all huddled around a propane lamp and pretended we were in a tent in the middle of a forest. Mom roasted marshmallows with her cigarette lighter, and Dad spun a story of spending a night in a tent in a forest and spotting a bear. He hadn't been scared—Dad would never admit to fear—but his tall tale seemed so real that we twins shivered. We scooted closer to him, Mom too, and he let us huddle around him. The lamp dimmed as the propane burned up. Only a pinpoint left, just before the dark closed in, he finally opened his arms and pressed us to his chest.

Artis turned from the window and said he had never hugged us in his life.

"It would be easier not to grieve for him if you believed that, wouldn't it?" I said. Easier to believe we hadn't lost something irretrievable by staying away. Easier not to wish we hadn't done it.

We rose from the table, holding our chairs for balance when in the past we would have held each other. Artis started to reach for me, whether to hug or hit, I wasn't sure, then changed her mind.

"He had beautiful handwriting," I said.

"Did not," she said.

"He could spell better than our teachers."

"Could not."

"How can we forgive ourselves?" I asked.

Artis replied, "You mean forgive him?"

We had called each other every day for years and years. We had whispered over the din of bossy babies and infantile supervisors. Through sickness and storms we had always carved a space to let the other in.

But that night we said no more.

Artis turned her music on and blocked me out. For once, I didn't know what she was listening to. We had always shared, an earbud each, before.

I could barely totter to bed, all my senses impaired. I caught glimmers, though: a street lamp through the bedroom window, the green light of a cell phone charging next to my son's bright head.

I'd expected not to see anything at all by myself.

36

The next morning, I woke with a headache. I had never wondered before if Paula had one, too. No matter how far away we lived from each other, I had always just known. Without her dreams in my head, mixing with mine, I had slept in fits.

Everything throbbed. I must have ground my teeth down to dust without my mouth guard on. My boobs were squeezed too tight in the sports bra I had been too drunk to take off.

In the living room, the boys, wide awake, hid under a card table draped with blankets. "Barack! Pablo!" Mom called. "Time for breakfast."

"We both have the same name now," they said. "Call us Barlo."

"Come on out," Mom said.

"Not yet," came a booming voice from their fort. "We're about to be born. This time, from the same belly."

Someone clanked plates in the kitchen. Could have been Paula, could have been anyone. Her every sound, every movement a foreign language now.

37

*A*rtis finally emerged from her room. "No run today?" I asked, but she ignored me. She was usually out of the house by six, a pool of sweat by 6:15.

But she might as well have been out of the country. There she was, belly-flopped on the floor, carpet burning her skin. Run? She could barely stand.

"Marco," I said.

Nothing.

I tapped my knee, the first phrase of a song I had written just for her. She had always tapped the second part. Before.

I stretched out beside her in child's pose. She scooted away, as if my "hocus pocus" might be catchy. That's what she called my yoga practice, but she used to do it with me anyway. *For* me, I realized now. But not anymore.

I thought we had connected during the night, but I realized that it had been a dream. Now her breathing and moving and thinking was nothing but white noise. Was this what life was like for singletons? I couldn't live a whole day this way.

I'll agree with whatever you say if you'll just come back.

But I couldn't form those words. My tongue was stuck behind my two front teeth. And she could no longer read my mind.

The boys ate funeral cake for breakfast, making chewing sounds they pretended came from the cars they rolled on their plates. They didn't touch their drinks. "Milk is for babies," they said.

"No fair Daddy gets milk," we had said so long ago, after we had seen him in bed with Mom and her naked breasts.

Now she slouched on the couch, staring at a telenovela. She didn't speak a word of Spanish.

At long last, we had Mom to ourselves. Wasn't that what we had wanted all along?

I had to get her out of the house. Away from the mac and cheese and sheet cakes oozing from Tupperware and overflowing from her fridge, the kindnesses of neighbors that turned the cramped kitchen into an extension of the funeral home. Crusted-over pans soaked in the sink. No matter how much we striped them with blue soap, they smelled like sympathy wreaths, sticky tissues, and wet salt.

I needed to get away from our baby pictures framed on the dressers. The dollhouse we had played with as kids, which Mom still used for the daycare babies. Dad's spelling bee plaque, displayed on the wall of the tiny master bedroom. His wolf teeth and beaver pelts and arrowheads.

I needed to get away from his guns in the safe, not nearly locked up enough, because I knew where he kept the key, in his underwear drawer. Taking Mom to breakfast was just an excuse.

I pulled a high-tech winter hat over my short slicked-back hair, which suddenly didn't feel short enough. A shaved head would have been better. A start over. "Coming with us?"

"I need some time alone." Artis had never said anything like that before.

Mom stopped tying her winter boot, as if the sound of the laces rubbing against each other had made her hear wrong. "What?"

Artis sat up and crossed her hands in front of her chest. Mom urged her to her feet, patted us both on the bottoms, scooted us along toward the front door, the way she had when we were tiny.

I threw my sister her coat, and she zipped into the down, the hood's fake fur swallowing her face. She had always followed me before without waiting to be asked.

Of course Mom wasn't hungry. "How about Fantasyland instead?" she asked, clicking into the shoulder belt as I started the car.

Artis climbed into the back and slammed more loudly than necessary.

"So much for global warming," Mom said. "It's been snowing here for months."

"This is what happens when ice caps melt." I waited for the windshield to defog. "Sometimes heat waves. Sometimes freakish storms that last forever."

Mom whipped her arms through the air. "I think it's your dad."

"I know. You said that at the funeral." I shot my sister a look that said, *our crazy parents,* a look we had perfected over the years. But Artis stared out the window, avoiding my eyes.

Then I drove south and made a wide right toward the rec center, where Mom said there was still a Fantasyland in the basement every Christmas season. Would a little nostalgia be good for her? It was worth a try. My rental swerved on the slippery roads, the sky a whiteout.

38

*P*aula, as always, drove like an old lady. Why had I let her take the wheel? Oh yeah, because my headache was turning into a fucking migraine. If migraines actually exist. Maybe this was just what it felt like to be cut off from her, my head spinning away from my shoulders.

We pulled into the empty parking lot. This "winter wonderland" had always been swarmed when we were kids. We would have to fight the crowds and wait in line. The latest blizzard must have kept everyone away. Maybe the place was closed due to weather.

No such luck.

We walked down to the basement, past the wooden Fantasyland sign. Everything looked exactly the same as it had twenty years ago. The same as twenty years before that, Mom said, when she was a kid. It was a world where no one had ever heard of computers. Let alone drones that could deliver packages or drop bombs on the same day.

From half a dozen glassed-in displays, animatronic dolls stared at us, creepy and silent, waiting for someone to press the start button so they could dance and sing.

Mom pressed the button on the "All I Want for Christmas Is My Two Front Teeth" display, and I knew that when the music began to seep out of the speakers, the gap-toothed little girl doll with blonde braids and a gingham dress would point to her mouth as her lips moved stiffly in sync with the words.

But the start button didn't start a thing.

Broken. Which might explain why no one was here.

At least we hadn't brought the boys. They didn't need to see the bursting seams on the doll's dress, the random unlit letters, the metal patches where a polar bear's fur had gone AWOL in the "White Christmas" display.

I used to think the dolls moved on their own. I used to think electricity was another name for magic. In other words, I didn't use to think.

Dad sure loved Christmas crap. He was so damn sentimental.

We all sat down on the bench in front of the glass case. Paula fidgeted. Mom pushed the button on "Two Front Teeth" again and again. She never gave up, did she?

Finally, she moved over and pressed the button for "Frosty the Snowman," and the song blasted from the speakers so loud we couldn't think.

When the song ended, I pressed the button again. Thinking is overrated.

39

*O*ur little guys needed to see this place. They were only five, and they already spent too much time with their screens. It was so simple, this mechanical technology. More . . . I don't know . . . authentic.

I said all that, but no one heard me, with Artis pressing buttons and playing songs at the volume of a siren. "Silver Bells." "Rudolph the Red-Nosed Reindeer." She knew we needed to talk to Mom.

I took a few deep breaths and one big *om*, and then I grabbed my sister's wrist to finally stop her.

If I had to hover there all day, covering the start button with my back so Artis wouldn't keep pressing it, I would.

"I'm sorry," I told Mom. I waited for Artis to join in, but she said nothing, digging her heels into the worn-down carpet and stuffing her hands deep into her pockets.

For the first time, I saw the pain carved into Mom's face for what it was: her mourning Dad's death, yes, but more than that, the grief *we* had caused her many years ago, by making believe Dad was already dead.

The squint lines around her eyes, the broken capillaries in her cheeks, the crush and hunch of her shoulders: We had done that to her body, hadn't we? Etched ourselves into her.

Mom shook her head, meaning what, I didn't know. That she didn't believe me? That it wasn't enough? That we wouldn't get off that easily? Side to side her chin swung, her mile-high hair drooping, starting, finally, to feel the tug of gravity.

I felt it, too, and began to collapse in on myself. It was too hard to do this alone. I sat and pressed the fake fur of my hood into my face, then hung my head so low I could have mopped the tile with my cropped hair.

40

hat Paula means is," I began. With her nose between her knees, she was in no position to contradict me. And Mom didn't know we couldn't speak for each other anymore.

"She's sorry you didn't visit your dad." Mom finished my sentence.

"No." No way in hell, I wanted to say, but the army had taught me to address my elders with respect. Damn, she was making it hard, though.

"You didn't return his phone calls or emails or texts, either," Mom said. "He threatened to drive up to campus and knock down your door, but I always stopped him."

As if she could block his way with her flimsy torso, holding him back with her spindly wrists.

"That's not what I want to talk about," I said. "There's something else. Paula's too chicken to tell you. She'll just write a song about it, all cryptic guitar riffs and pretentious electric violin, and you'll have to guess, along with all her fans, which parts of the song really happened." I sat up straight, like the statue of Winged Victory but in a tight sports bra. "Wild Pete knows. He said it last night: *So you're the girls who killed your dad.*"

"I heard," Mom said. "But he didn't mean it."

"Why would he say it then?"

"People go crazy at funerals. Like Ya-Ya. Remember what she said?"

"When Papu died? But she was right. That's the point. Dad *did* kill his dad. You told us."

"I told you what?" Mom said. "Papu had a stroke. Everyone knew."

"In college we texted you and asked if what she said was true, and you didn't respond."

"I never got that text," Mom said.

"You didn't say no." I rubbed my eyes to soften the throbbing in my head. Instead I just dislodged a lash. Who knew they could be so sharp? "We thought that meant yes."

Mom raised her voice, maybe the first time ever. She had to wait till he was gone to find her inner tiger? "If there's one thing I taught you," she said, "one thing I thought I was doing right by my girls, it's that no always means no, and only yes means yes."

Dad really didn't kill Papu. Of course not. How could we have imagined he could do such a thing? Purple dots flashed in front of my eyes, then two sharp lines. Was this really a migraine or just a hangover? The shapes blurred into gumdrops blooming on our little legs, his elbows ramming into her ribs. We never knew if he would some-day go too far.

Another reason we believed he could kill? Because *we* could.

"I'm glad Ya-Ya was wrong," I finally said. "But Wild Pete was right."

"Don't listen to him. He spends so much time in the woods, he's like an animal," Mom said.

"No. That night you called us, we wanted to come. But we couldn't, not with Dad there. So we wished he was dead. And then you called and said he was."

Mom let out a sigh that echoed all the way to the North Pole.

That sigh made me feel small again. I pulled my feet up onto the bench, looped my arms around my shins, rested my chin on my knees. Paula barely managed to pull her head and torso up. She sucked in her lips, then opened her mouth.

41

I . . ." The word felt sharp against my tongue. I didn't like saying it. "I didn't mean to."

Mom peeled off her coat, pushed Artis and me together, and placed her hands on both of our thighs. "It's not your fault your dad died."

"You think we didn't know our own power?" I plucked a vial of essential oil from my pocket and inhaled long and deep. Lavender for tranquility.

"You didn't do it." Mom sat still as a picture, even as Artis bristled at her touch. "It's not possible."

"You don't need to humor us," I said. "We know what we're capable of."

She sounded too calm, almost robotic. "You didn't kill your dad—" She removed her hands from us and steepled them in prayer. Her eyes ticked back and forth between us.

"You don't understand—" I said.

"—because I did."

My sister and I turned toward each other and then back toward Mom. We both bit down hard on our fingers at exactly the same time. In sync again for a second, glazed eyes staring at Mom. We could have chomped through the bone and not felt a thing.

42

What. The. Frick. Frack. Paddywack. All those years in the army, and that was the best expletive I could come up with, and even that only in my head. All that bubbled from my mouth was a moan. Something like "Moooooom." At least I managed to make it sound obscene.

"It's not easy," Mom said. "*This*, what I'm doing now, telling you about it. *This*, the thing I did, a few days ago."

Her words echoed off the walls, amplified by each crack in the paint. "Let me squeeze in here with you," she said. She pushed between us as insistently as she'd pushed us together only a few minutes earlier.

I couldn't have moved on my own if I had wanted to, not my ass or my big mouth. Her monologue, a medusa, turned me to stone.

"I couldn't tell you yesterday, at the church," she said. "Or on the phone. People wouldn't understand."

I stared at the patterns of light and dark on the ceiling, cupping my chin. Paula laced both hands over her face, squinting through fingers.

It was just last Saturday morning, Mom explained,

when Wild Pete rang the doorbell. I could almost see him, second-skinned in ski pants and face mask, hail pounding as he pushed the door shut behind him, his stomp on the mat speckling Mom's black ballet slippers and floor-length purple nightgown with slush.

Dad still lay in bed. He had been sick and tired, and the weather stirred up outside was anything but welcoming, but he insisted on hunting down a tree for Christmas. Pete had brought his axe. Ever since he had moved back down to the lower forty-eight, years after we left for school, he and Dad had spent every spare moment out in the elements, again.

Pete swatted Mom on the ass. She wanted to slap him back, hard, but she stopped herself, balancing carefully so the steaming mug she had poured for Dad wouldn't spill and burn her hands. The hands she would need to keep steady later that day.

Pete had always been sweet on her. Dad wasn't the only one who called her "goddess." "Didn't you know that?" she asked Paula and me. We shook our heads. So she'd humor Pete for the day. Just so he would go along with their plan.

Mom brought Dad his coffee and helped him dress. Flannel and jeans, no coat or boots, his skin too thick for that. He was sweating, already, in his sleeveless undershirt.

He tried to scoop her up and carry her over the threshold out of the bedroom, then fell to the floor. "Promise?" he asked.

She nodded from the waist up. "I'll get those girls home. You just pick a big fat tree, and I'll decorate the house for them." Mom parted the blackout drapes and waved through the living room window as they left, her tiny hands half-swallowed by the gauzy curtains beneath, the two men bathed in blinking colored lights.

In minutes, Pete's truck had already gathered a second sleeve of frost. Dad brushed it off with gloveless hands, then both men jumped into the cab, carving a tunnel with the vehicle through the white fog. The pickup shrank in the distance—a clown car, a windup toy.

It was the weekend, so Sunflower was closed, and she was alone. No plastic *T. rexes* roared from chubby toddler hands. No diapers leaked onto her lap as she bottle-fed and stroked and swayed and put to bed the babies warm as little overheated engines.

That long day, the longest of Mom's life, she roasted beef and baked gingerbread. She hung lights and cut out paper snowflakes.

Dad and Pete drove hours into the country and hours back. The tree they brought back barely fit through the door, but Pete heaved it in.

Then Mom called us one last time. Called us the way she did every holiday. Begged us to come, but we were too busy. Always busy with something, weren't we? she said to Paula and me. Changing our addresses or our clothes or our minds. No, she corrected herself. We never changed our minds.

Our poor mom. Hadn't we said that all our lives? Her tone now implied that we were the problem. But in the army, standing by your convictions is called being strong.

That morning she had promised Dad she would bring us home. Only one way left to make that happen. Mom signaled to Wild Pete. "It's time."

But Pete didn't move. That self-described grizzly man, the Alaskan Paul Bunyan, scaler of Mount McKinley, wrestler of rams, tamer of mountain lions—he chickened out. Though he knew Mom would cover for him, he didn't have the guts to make the gun go off "by accident." Happened more and more, guns shrinking so small they were often mistaken for phones. Pete ducked out the door with nothing more than a bear hug good-bye—a slap on Dad's back, a squeeze to Mom's thigh. He held it all in while Dad was looking. His face tightened with the effort. Mom knew as soon as he drove out of sight he would pull over on the shoulder. And let it all out.

Mom and Dad ate beef and potatoes and gingerbread that night. Then went to bed.

His chest rose and fell, the air from his mouth audible and visible, its wheezing and misting a movie she never tired of. She watched him for hours, remembering every night they had spent together. Sleeping. And not.

She smelled and tasted him. Wet moss. Hot embers. Sweet sweat and smoky breath.

She lived through their entire marriage like a waking dream. And then she did it.

"What's the first thing he taught you?" she asked us. "Once you were old enough to understand?"

We still didn't speak. I didn't dare open my mouth for fear this was a dream and I would wake up and never hear the end of the story. I lowered my eyes to my knees.

"It's the first thing he taught me, too."

How to control life and death, no weapons required. The most important thing he had learned in the army. Not a technique from Ranger training. More like something from one of the myths Ya-Ya used to read to us from ancient Greece.

Mom put on her gloves, then pressed on his throat. A gentle thumb, not enough pressure to wake him, directly on the spot he had showed us on our tenth birthday, during our hike in the forest. The artery that connects our hearts to our brains. The spot that, if blocked, takes your breath away. Doesn't require much strength. You can do it in the middle of the night, and no one will ever know it was anything other than sleep apnea.

A thumb on his throat—soft, quiet, peaceful. Quick and painless. A pause in the middle of a dream. He had just stopped breathing.

The perfect crime. The only problem was that I hadn't thought of it myself.

43

*B*ut—" I said. Maybe Artis did, too. Maybe the dolls and the snowmen and the penguins in the Christmas displays behind glass joined in. Maybe the whole room had learned to speak again.

Mom made a stop sign with her hand and said she couldn't have said this on the phone. These days every line was hacked. Then she tried to explain.

She had promised Dad she would do it. He wanted her to. She didn't think she could, so she had asked Wild Pete to do it instead, to persuade Dad to settle for an accident with a firearm.

When they went to bed that night, Dad told her: It's the only way to end this endless winter.

She called it mercy killing. Assisted suicide. That's how she thought of her deed. He had told her back when he was well that if he ever lost his mind, he didn't want his body to stick around. She thought he had told us when the doctors had diagnosed him a year ago. Maybe he had. We hadn't read his emails or texts in what felt like millennia. And when Mom had mentioned his name, Artis and I both pretended we couldn't hear. Though I did write those songs for him, didn't I?

Dad might have been sick even when we were kids, the doctors told Mom. It's hard to diagnose at first. It gets worse and worse over time. Makes you lose your memory little by little until you can't take care of yourself. Even makes you mean. That's the worst of it.

Lewy Body Syndrome. A kind of early-onset dementia. People end up in nursing homes before they're old enough to retire.

Would we have believed her if she had told us earlier? She thought she had. She had always said we should give Dad some slack, but she had been saying that since we were teenagers.

She didn't believe the doctors anyway. The explanation she preferred was this: climate change. "That's what did him in." In the old days, he really had controlled the weather, she explained. He was more than human.

I could remember when he had made it rain, when he had brought down thunder and lightning and snow. He had made spring come when he wanted it to. He did have that power.

Then he didn't anymore. The world stopped working the way it had for so many thousands of years. Weather no longer predictable. Sea levels rose. Ice caps melted. Tornadoes on the Oregon coast? New Orleans sinking into the sea? "These things were not your Dad's doing," Mom said. His power was slipping. And it drove him crazy. Literally.

"Doctors always have an explanation," she continued. "Melancholia? Call it depression and take a chill pill. Visions? Those are hallucinations, the wrong chemicals in your brain. All those prophets in the Bible who saw God in the bushes would be packed away in the psychiatric ward today."

So she chose to believe what Dad told her himself: That he couldn't die. That all he could do was leave the Earth and go back up to the sky. There, he would be himself again. He was done here. A body was just a costume he slipped on for a little while and took off again when it was time.

"Remember what I said at the funeral?" Mom's voice hushed so low I could hear her tears. "The snow out the window, that was your dad. I can feel him. He's happy again. He's so glad you girls finally came home for Christmas."

I opened my mouth, and only air emerged. Artis couldn't even move. Her bones must have turned to rock. The clocks stopped.

What was my sister thinking? Why wouldn't she even look at me? I could tell her face was stuck in a smirk behind the hands that covered half her face.

The animated dolls had nothing to say after all. What were we doing here? The coffee that was all I could swallow for breakfast burned through my guts. I tried to visualize the acid neutralizing, a stormy sea calming, the way my meditation teacher had taught me. I couldn't throw up now. Artis needed me, even if she was too proud to admit it. I zipped my long coat up above my mouth and panted into the fluffy down to let the carbon dioxide settle me. Then I covered my face with my hands and disappeared. I tasted my saliva, the raw rust in the back of my throat.

Whatever we called what Mom had done, Dad was gone. I would never, ever see him again. He would never see my husband. Never meet my son. The past was gone, but so was the future, thanks to Mom's thumb. My head hung so heavy in my hands. Snot slipped through the cracks between my fingers.

In the end he was felled by a hundred-pound woman. That didn't make sense. Or maybe it did. In a way, this was still just Mom being Mom. She had never been able to say no to him. From the time she was sixteen going on twelve, she had said yes.

I tapped a rhythm on my knees, starting a phrase for my sister to finish on hers. But she didn't seem to hear it.

"What I'm trying to say," Mom said, "is that your dad had special powers, so he lived by special rules."

Artis started to laugh, a dismissive sound like the caw of a dozen birds. A murder of crows.

"You didn't see the lightning he made at our fourteenth birthday party?" I asked her. "What about how he zapped all the cyberstalkers who went after the Slutty Twins, with bolts that shook the internet? And every year, remember, he—not The Groundhog—made spring? Did you go through childhood with your eyes closed?"

"One of us did," she said, "but it wasn't me. You're as deluded as he was."

"Maybe delusion is another word for love."

We argued this way, back and forth, voices muffled by our coats, while Mom left to clean the salty red blotches from her face in the bathroom. Even though (or especially because) she was the cause of Dad's death, she was still a grieving widow.

When Mom emerged, her hair unraveled and her jewelry tangled in it, she said, "I never meant to tell you what I did that night. It would have been safer for you not to know."

"I thought that's why you brought us here," I said.

"No, you brought me. And I know why. You wanted to ask about Zeke."

"Who?"

"I saw you talking to him at the funeral," she said. "He gave you his card."

The guy in the purple tie. "Who is he?" I asked. But then I knew.

The guy with the pointy chin just like ours, that couldn't be hidden even under facial hair. The guy who looked so much like us. Of course. He had been trying to tell us, hadn't he? He said, "Call me Zeke. My family calls me Zeke."

"*My family.*"

Our brother.

My sister knew, too. I could tell by the way her smirk tightened into clenched cheeks. She shot up from her seat and bolted out the door.

Mom sprang up after her, but I blocked the way. "Let her run it out," I said.

Mom slunk back to her bench. "She's always been such a hothead. Reminds me of someone else I know." She wasn't looking at me, Artis's identical twin, but up at the sky, out the window.

"Only way she can think is to move. Let her sweat through this. She'll forgive Dad, with time."

"Forgive him for Zeke?" Mom asked.

"And other things," I said. "For busting our butts."

"You mean discipline," Mom said.

"For abandoning us in the woods."

"That's how you learned to navigate." Blink blink blink. She was at it again.

"For reducing your grocery money if you weighed too much."

"He was helping me with my diet."

"For never letting us go on a sleepover."

"Because you didn't try to win the spelling bee. He wanted to teach you to be ambitious. And it worked."

"For storming into our room and breaking everything in sight."

"He'd just lost his job."

"We might even forgive him for making you scream behind your bedroom door at night."

"You mean when we were making love?" Mom stood up. A tiny curlicue of a grin rose up to her beauty mark. "How is that any of your business?"

"Dad walked into the hall and kicked us."

"He nudged you with his feet." Mom kneaded her earlobe. "And you know. You were sometimes in the way."

"She may even forgive you for not protecting us." I paused. This was the hardest thing for me to say. "Or she may not."

"If I had," Mom said, "how would you ever have learned to protect yourselves?"

44

I grabbed the key from Paula's purse, then dashed through the snow globe the world had become. Had. To. Get. Out. My throat clogged with rage and mucus. My toes frozen in slushy boots.

But the rental lay immobile in a mountain of snow. This weather was a lion escaped from the zoo, fiercer and hungrier every season. I yanked a shovel from the trunk and began to dig. Dad could shovel shirtless. I could shovel with my bare hands if I had to.

What could Zeke do? What kind of hide did he have? Thin as a coddled child's. Now I knew who this man was.

Heave, dump, heave, dump.

He was the boy Dad gave our birthday presents to. Our Hamster Hotel. He was the one who got a pet when all we got was a gun. The gun I wished I had in my hands right now, so I could shoot something.

Pitch. Chuck. Hurl. Was this a shovel or a spoon? An ice pick would help more.

He was the son Dad meant when he said, "The two of you don't add up to one boy." I could beat him in a brawl. Outman the little geek with the ugly purple tie.

He was the mysterious friend Dad had given his moose cap to, that day we had seen them at Downriver Chik-N. The boy we worried Dad loved. The boy he did love, but not the way we thought.

Scrape. Crack. Fling.

He wasn't a boy anymore. He was taller than us, almost as old as we were. Shoulders that stretched for miles. When he was young, I hadn't noticed his hair, dark as a dog's nose. So black it glinted blue. Didn't see that he had Dad's chin.

My chin. My eyes. My hair. Of course he did.

The air polka-dotted with snow, but through the white, I spotted Paula and Mom, trudging toward me.

"What the hell?" Paula said. "You just disappeared. I didn't even realize you took the car key."

"You knew where I was." As soon as I said it, though, I realized it was a lie. I might as well have been speaking Uzbekistani. How had it gotten so cold out here all of a sudden? As frozen as an empty stare.

"Let's go," Mom said. "Before you have to dig us out again."

I opened the passenger door for her. Paula slid into the back, then did her signature silent squirm. She never said much, did she? All our lives I had to do the talking for both of us.

"Who is he, anyway?" I couldn't even look Mom in the eye. Luckily, I didn't have to, since if I did, we would crash. "Pixie's kid?"

"You remember her?" Mom said, her eyes sliding away from the diamond stud in my ear.

"Were there others?" My hands hurt from squeezing the steering wheel so tight.

Mom did her weird syncopated blinking thing, the tic that had embarrassed me most about her as a kid, and said, "Don't look at me like *I* did something wrong."

I could hear Paula sucking in her lips, like she was going to swallow her whole face, like she was some kind of jellyfish. Like she had forgotten how to talk.

"How could you?" I hit the gas too hard and slid all the way through a red light. I didn't want to stop anyway. "How could you call him our brother?"

"He's a good man," Mom said. "And your dad, he did the honorable thing. He acknowledged his son's existence."

"Not to us." The visibility was for shit. If I opened my eyes wider, though, I could cut through the snow. I could make out every crystal, each "unique" flake. I knifed through the lanes.

"He didn't want to hurt you," Mom said.

I tried not to laugh.

"But you heard Ya-Ya's awful words at Papu's funeral: *You and your bastard son,* she said. *That's what killed him.* Everyone heard it. She meant the shame had caused a stroke. She may have even believed it. If you didn't close your ears, you had to hear her say it."

"Dad was the bastard. How could you stay with him?"

"I tried to leave. You didn't really think I went to the hospital for 'nerves,' did you?"

"You always came back."

"No one else could satisfy me. Or train you girls."

"Train us for what?"

"To get what you want. To want it so much you make it so. To be like him."

"Let's hope we're not, for our husbands' sake. For our boys."

"You know what I mean."

"Thick-skinned?"

"He knew that was the only way."

"Did he have other kids?"

"No."

"That you know of. What an ass."

"Having a kid makes you an ass?" Mom said. "I guess you'd rather not exist."

"I guess." Let her think I was that reckless. Me, the one steering the car.

"Where are you going?" Mom asked.

She'd like to know, wouldn't she? She'd like to have all the answers. Now she knew what it felt like.

Forty. Fifty. Sixty miles an hour. Didn't matter which direction as long as I merged onto the highway. Finally up to seventy-five. I could lift my foot and glide for miles.

"I was just a kid when I had you," Mom said. "People said I shouldn't have. But not your dad. He wouldn't let me get rid of you. He wouldn't let Pixie get rid of Zeke. Didn't want to let you, either."

"Let me what? Have an abortion? I thought you were on our side. Dad punished you for taking us to the clinic. Remember?"

"Sometimes he got angry. We all have flaws. But he loved us. He loved us all." Every time she said the *L* word, my nose ran. "Love is not a pizza. You don't slice it up and then it's gone."

"You read that on a fortune cookie?"

"Remember how he called me Goddess?" Her tapping foot and blinking eyes stilled; her forehead unclenched. She smiled for the first time since I had arrived from the airport. She smiled so wide I had to see even when I tried not to look. She wound her hair around and around into a crown. The lily tattoo on the back of her neck shone white. Her teeth gleamed.

In my head, I was seventeen again, and Mom was walking to the grocery store, after Dad had sold the Bull to buy the tow truck. What did she think of that? Had grief just whitewashed her memory?

I pushed away thoughts of Pixie and Dad in bed. I didn't want to remember how, when I had met Pixie the first time, I had fantasized about having her as a big sister. Those alluring leopard-skin stilettos. Her soft cleavage and hard studs. The diamonds Paula and I now wore in our ears. "Why are we only finding out about this now?

"Your dad didn't want you to know."

"And you just did whatever he said? You just rolled over for him, didn't you? Always. Like a dog."

My sister finally moved. She leaned up from the back seat, and her voice slid between Mom and me. She whispered, "Just stop."

I moved into the fast lane. We were hydroplaning, but I didn't care.

"You don't know what you're talking about," Mom said. "Zeke was an accident like you girls were. And Moose took care of us."

I needed a mint to clear my palate, but all I could fish out of my pocket was trash. "How can you act so fucking calm? When you've been betrayed and lied to for so long?"

Then my sister clasped her hand behind my neck. She squeezed it the way we used to squeeze each other's knees. I knew what it meant, even though I could no longer read her mind. Mom wasn't the one who was lied to, Paula said, with the pad of her middle finger circling the knot of my scapula. *We were.*

And yet she still thought we should forgive him.

I pulled onto the shoulder, stopped, and pressed my forehead against the wheel. Then I yanked the diamond out of my earlobe and dumped it into the cupholder. I would have dropped it into an ashtray full of ashes, had there been one.

45

*M*om pressed the emergency lights. I opened my sister's door and webbed my hands over hers, still on the wheel. They were as hot as her temper, but I soon cooled them down. Knuckle to knuckle, joint to joint. The fate lines of our palms stacked. Without me, I wondered if Artis would burn up in an hour.

Whenever I needed to turn on my brain again, I walked or soaked in Epsom salts. There were no bathtubs on the interstate, so I took over the wheel, turned on cruise control, and let the car do the walking, farther and farther, till I finally found words for my sister. "You heard what Mom did to Dad. And all you want to talk about is Zeke?"

"At least I said something," Artis said. "You were zoned out on your phone."

"Googling Lewy Body Syndrome. It's an often-misdiagnosed brain disease," I explained. "The second most common dementia after Alzheimer's. Starts young. Typically hits after fifty but sometimes much earlier. Can cause impaired thinking. Visual hallucinations. Mood and behavior changes. Delusions or paranoia. Who knows how long this thing had been hijacking his personality?"

"The doctors *said* he had it. That doesn't mean he had it," Mom corrected.

Artis kicked my seat, the way toddlers do on airplanes. "An accidental asshole is still an asshole," she said.

For a moment, I thought she was talking about herself.

46

I could Google, too. Better to look at my phone than remind myself that Paula couldn't drive. A dusting of snow and you have to crawl below the speed limit? I could fly a copter through a sandstorm with a bullet wound better than this.

LBD. That's what the internet called it. The Little Black Dress of brain disorders. Lewy Body Dementia. Lacking Better Descriptions. Let's Be Dumb. "It's hereditary," I read on my screen.

"Can be," Paula said, her eyes fixed on the taillights directly ahead.

"There's a gene. You have to pull up the research. See?" I leaned between my sister and mom to show them.

"I can't look. We'll crash," Paula said.

"As slow as this, I think we can risk it," I said.

"What are our chances?"

"As much as one in two."

"Either me or you."

Or Zeke, neither of us said.

Let it be him. Did my sister think that, too? Could I make her? Could I think a thing and make it so? Had we ever been able to? I could close my eyes and try.

My phone buzzed. Sebastian wanted to know when we were coming home. What in God's name, he asked, were we doing out in this storm?

"We" were doing nothing. Paula was driving. I was surfing. Mom was staring up at the agitating clouds, her own silent movie.

Maybe that wasn't true. Maybe we were all thinking the same word without saying it: *Zeke.*

"He said he wouldn't contact you," Mom said. "But you could contact him."

Paula pounded a tune on the steering wheel and hummed in harmony. Then she said, "I already did."

47

*H*ours later, I answered Mom's door and saw a ghost. Big eyes, endless chest, the chin that could double as a weapon.

Snow melted from his face, his thin, clumpy beard. When he took off his puffy coat, he shrank to human size.

Zeke. Of course it was. Who had I thought it would be? I had invited him.

"Come in!" Mom said, her voice a forced chirp.

The husbands shook hands with this stranger, this family member, this half-this and half-that, then rushed outside to shovel snow. Mom hung up Zeke's coat while he stomped his shoes clean.

Artis tilted her head, a hint of a nod, her fingers burrowed deep in her pockets. I felt my sister's glare, daring me to withhold my hand, too. I had always obeyed that stare, and look where it had gotten me. So I reached out my arms to see how Zeke would respond. He folded me in his embrace, and I disappeared into his familiar smell, the musky oil Dad had used to groom his beard. I could hear the boys building a blanket fort in our old bedroom, clicking their tongues as triggers.

Mom offered leftover funeral cake and her homemade gingerbread men, but Zeke seemed too fidgety to sit. He wore a ski cap the same color as his dark hair, skateboard shoes despite the snow, and a baggy T-shirt under an unbuttoned faded flannel. Without his skinny purple tie, he fit right in with the decor.

Our silence echoed off the taxidermy decorations and made our sons' chatter all the more audible. Now they were pretending their bodies were made of smartphones. Whenever they wanted to call someone, they just flicked their fingers. They were so high-tech, they could even call the dead.

"How's heaven?" they asked in their child voice.

Then they pretended to speak for Dad. "Heaven is good," they made him say in a boom like God.

"You're not lonely?" they asked in their high-pitched squeak.

"Han Solo is here," said the booming voice. "And Luke Skywalker."

"Is there lots of candy?"

"Every day is Halloween. But I never get sick to my stomach."

"Do you have a stomach?"

"No, I'm made of snow."

Then, finally, both boys in stereo: "Do you miss us?"

No answer. I squeezed my shoulders into a hunch up to my chin then peeked around the room. Everyone else was staring at their phones. I seemed to be the only one who could hear a thing.

No answer still from the bedroom.

Then finally a shout so loud even Mom heard. "No!" She scuffled away to close their door.

None of us knew what to say, so Mom gave us something to do. We helped her carry boxes from the basement. Photos, clothes, and treasures. Dad's knives and trophies and gear. Each box weighed me down to the ground. Artis lugged two at a time, as if they were empty.

Zeke marched through the house, silently marveling. At the animal parts on the walls, the coffee table Dad had built in high school shop class. I tried to ignore the frayed edges of furniture, the cracked paint and stained carpet. I could have bought my parents a new couch with the money from my latest record, at least.

"I always wanted to come inside." Someone finally spoke. It was Zeke. He sat at the kitchen table and accepted a cup of coffee from Mom.

I joined him, dropping boxes at his feet. Mom pushed a plate of cookies toward me, and I nibbled on one just to be polite. "You could have asked."

"Dad said no." It took me a minute to realize who he meant. Moose. Shouldn't Zeke have called him by another name? Something that meant half dad? Though he wasn't, was he? Zeke had seen Dad more than we had as adults, for sure.

"He thought you'd stopped talking to him because . . ." Zeke stared up at the moose antlers above the TV, the ones I secretly believed were deer. He paused so long I thought he must be waiting for the animal to tell him what to say. "Because you found out about me."

"We didn't know you existed," I said.

"But you saw me at that chicken place."

I had told him that on the phone. "We didn't know who you were then." Did we?

"Then why?"

I excavated a wolf tooth necklace from one of the boxes we had carried up and added it to Zeke's pile. Why had I stopped talking to Dad? How many times had I been asked that question? By my friends and my husband, therapists and strangers, even in music magazine interviews. "It's complicated," I always said. But now I knew it was simply this: because my sister told me to.

I couldn't say that, so I turned up my palms.

48

e had reasons," I said. I didn't want to talk to Zeke. I didn't even want him here. Couldn't he tell by the evil eye I shot in his direction? But Paula's mouth had run out of battery again. Someone had to respond.

"What did he do to you?" Zeke asked.

"What didn't he?" I moved the gingerbread men around on my plate. I finally understood why Mom played with her food instead of eating it.

"I want to know everything," Zeke said.

"Why?" I plucked the raisin eyes.

"You had the life I wanted," he said.

"You have no idea." I tore off the arms, the legs, and the head.

He leaned toward me, elbows on the table. "Then tell me."

I exhaled a loud puff of air and made my hands into pointy triangles. "We used to listen in the hall on the other side of our parents' door." And with those words I began to share my first memories. "Dad kicked us," I concluded. "So hard we had to wear long pants to cover up our bruises the next day."

I told him more. We were ten again, abandoned in the woods, bait for bears.

Fourteen, excavating shards from our skin, the glass from the picture frames Dad had knocked from our dressers shattered across the floor.

We were seventeen, and he said, "I'll get your tubes tied."

"Look what he did *for* you." Mom had been hovering at the sink, but now she sat down. "Look what he made you into. Fine young women."

Zeke said, "Dad taught you how to play guitar and sing. He told me that. He would have taught me, too, if we'd had time. Not just a weekend here or there, when he could pretend to be hunting."

I should have known those trips were fake. He never brought home meat.

"I always wanted . . ." Zeke slipped off his cap and pulled his cascade of hair back and secured it with a rubber band.

"You can have all his stuff," I said.

"I always wanted . . ." He stabbed his own thumb with a wolf tooth. "I followed you, you know. Walking home from school. I hid in a bush and watched you rehearse in your garage. I saw you at the spelling bee. At talent shows. I saw every clip of the Slutty Twins."

The pervy Peeping Tom. "I didn't know you were there."

"Maybe there's a lot you didn't know," he said.

Mom brought a second plate of cookies, to replace the men we had reduced to crumbs. Only Zeke refilled his plate. I mashed my crumbs to sand, then piled them into a hill.

"What about when he nursed you from pneumonia?" Mom asked. "When he read to you for hours on end? When he cooked you grilled cheese with olive oil and freshly picked dandelion greens?"

What did a dandelion green even look like?

"It's more convenient for you to remember only the things that fit your story," Mom said. "The story that justifies what you did."

What *we* did? What about her? But I couldn't say that. Not in front of Zeke. She could give a million selfless reasons, but even if they were true, what she did wasn't legal. She could prove nothing. Since Dad had no living will, if Zeke turned her in, she could even go to jail.

49

he story that justified what we did. When had Mom ever been so eloquent? Never. Or maybe I just hadn't listened.

In college I had waited for Dad to arrive at our dorm and beg us to take him back, to forgive him. Now I knew that forgiveness was a quiet thing. I didn't need to say the words aloud. Wherever else he was, Dad was also in my head.

He could finally read my mind. Like a twin.

He could hear me say with my eyes, "You can talk to me now. I'm sorry I didn't let you before." My words rose up to the clouds, and the sky responded in kind. Who knew lightning and thunder could occur in the middle of a snowstorm? We all looked out the window. The dog in the yard yipped and yapped the way he had whenever Dad came home.

Finally, Mom rose and herded us all to the basement. We watched her unlock each safe and hand us Dad's rifles one by one. "Take whichever you want," she said. "They're not loaded."

We all let out nervous laughs.

50

I knew which one, of course. I was the only person in the house who knew a thing about guns. I saw it right away, the twin of the one Dad had given us for our birthday way back when. Why had he only given us one?

I grabbed it and sequestered myself from their awkward chatter, letting the gun tell me where to go, landing on the spot where Dad had taught us to play guitar. A lot of good that did me in the army. Then I stripped down to bare feet on the cold concrete. I could hear the buzz against my soles and nothing else. We sank into Dad's chair—the gun and I. Cold metal woke my warm skin. All I could see were the insides of my eyelids.

I was thirteen again, rummaging in Dad's underwear drawer for the ammo, convincing Paula not to stop me, then aiming out the window. My skin prickly and hot, the blood coursing between my legs where new fur grew, my head filled with the power of the budding curves of my hips, the curved shaft in my hand.

I was nineteen again, spied on as I bathed in the lake, swimming to the bank to grab the gun and roust the Peeping Tom from the bushes like a startled deer. What had

Zeke said? That he had followed us all our lives. He was no better than that creep.

I closed my eyes and disappeared. I hadn't forgotten the way Dad had taught us how, in the woods, so long ago. I stilled my breath, calmed my bladder, moved as little as I could. Quiet as a dead man.

I let the gun speak to me. This is what it said:

Maybe it was Zeke's fault Dad never got to meet our husbands and sons. Maybe we *did* know about our "brother" all along. In the back of our minds, he could have been there, even if we hadn't wanted to acknowledge him.

"*Maybe* is a weak word," Dad would have said. Did say, just now. I could hear him in the cold metal, which sounded the same as the rattle of my brain. It felt good not to have to rely on only my own words, like a pathetic singleton. His voice echoed in my head: "Maybe is a half-assed idea. Maybe is a coward. Maybe is what you say when you refuse to take a stand. Maybe won't get you anywhere anytime soon."

Maybe was that limbo space I didn't want to keep falling into.

The gun had no patience for maybes. It made me say what I couldn't have said all those years but must have always known. That we didn't cut Dad off because he killed his dad. Or because he grounded us. The real reason was standing in the basement here with me, wearing an open flannel and a baggy T-shirt with the logo of his company, Phantom Limbs.

And there was the diamond stud in his ear, identical to the one my sister wore. Had she dug it out of the cupholder in the car and given it to him? Or had he stolen it? I said I didn't want it, but she had to know that wasn't what I meant. She had always known before. Before Zeke.

That diamond stud was everything.

The little thief.

I wanted to point the muzzle at him. The guns weren't loaded, so what did it matter?

The guns weren't loaded, Mom had *said*. She had also said "cardiac arrest" on the phone.

Anyway, I knew where Dad kept his cartridges. I could find my way to the underwear drawer and back before anyone knew I was gone. I could pretend to go to the bathroom. To check on the boys.

We had no special powers, did we, Paula and I? But the object I held in my hands did, its barrel gleaming, its oiled metal hard and stubborn. Ready? Aim.

Open your eyes.

And lay the gun down.

I couldn't kill anyone. Not as a civilian, anyway. Dad couldn't, either. I should have known that long ago. Paula and I were so like him. Nothing but cowards. Mom was the only one with any guts.

Imagine that.

How long had I sequestered myself down here? I had never been this alone before. Where was my sister? I didn't know how to not know where my sister was. And that voice I had just heard? Was it stuck in the gun? Or outside, in the sky, like Mom said?

Dad? Can you hear me?

Where do we go when we die? Where would I go? Who would offer me mercy if I inherited your demented gene? If I lost my mind early? Maybe I was losing it already.

Maybe? That voice again.

I fell to my knees on the concrete.

Then I heard laughter outside. That's where they all must have gone. I scraped myself from the floor and went to find my twin. Out the basement window, I saw them. She was with Zeke, and I didn't want to have to talk to him. Ever again. So I stood on my tiptoes and squinted at them through the murky glass.

51

A snowman needs a hat, so I gave him mine, the kind I wear on the subway when I want to go incognito. But the boys said no, Grandpa wouldn't wear a beanie like a hipster. That's what they called him. Grandpa.

"Where's my mom?" Pablo asked.

"She'll be back soon." I couldn't tell him she had disappeared. Let him think she was doing some last-minute shopping.

My brother went inside and ferreted a fur-lined earflap hat from one of the boxes from the basement. One of Dad's souvenirs from his hunting trips in Alaska. "Perfect," the boys said, though snowmen don't have ears.

A snowman needs mittens, too, at least in Michigan. I slipped mine over the prongs at the ends of the branch arms. My favorites. Puffy black like boxing gloves. But on the palms shone rainbow peace signs.

Pablo said his mom had a matching pair. "I love how you and my mom buy the same stuff even when you don't go shopping together. I love how you . . ."

Barack finished his cousin's sentence. ". . . read each other's minds."

I didn't have the heart to tell them I had picked out my sister's pair. That I always bought two of everything, then sent one to her.

Colson and Sebastian finished shoveling the sidewalks and the driveway and joined us in the yard. Mom opened her kitchen window. "Come back in! You'll catch your death!"

"We're not cold," the boys said. They took off their mittens to prove their point and packed snowballs with their bare hands. "We're robots."

"Won't you rust?" Mom asked.

"Grandpa's out here in the snow," they said. "He can't come in or he'll melt. And we don't want to leave him alone."

Mom tramped out in her ankle-length down. "Where's Artis?" she asked me.

"I don't know," I whispered. I couldn't believe I could not know everything about her and still breathe.

Zeke removed his flannel and tied it around the snowman's waist.

"Who's that guy with the beard, again?" the boys asked.

"He's Zeke," I said. "Your uncle Zeke."

"Will he die, too?" they asked. "Is that what grown-ups do?"

"No," I said. "Not right away."

"At least we got to meet him first," they said. "At least once."

"You'll see him again," I said. "I promise."

They pelted him with snowballs, and he faked a slow, dramatic death. Then they laughed. Did they even know what death meant?

We all got down on the ground, rolled onto our backs and flapped our arms, and said we were making snow puppies.

"Snow angels," Mom corrected us.

"How come everyone always looks up at the sky?" the boys asked. "Are the aliens coming?"

Let them. We could make room.

Flakes hung from our chins like beards. Mom gazed up at the clouds that kept dumping down on us. We breathed in the good and bad weather, and it mixed up inside us. We grabbed hands and huddled together. With so many bodies, we could stay warm.

52

*E*ven my husband didn't come looking for me. I heard him say that word: uncle. "Here's a snowball to throw at your uncle Zeke." I hadn't told my son that Zeke was his uncle. Is family so cheap it can be made in a day? *Here, knock Zeke down with an iceball,* I would have said. *Make a bruise. That's how he'll know you're family.*

I told Sebastian at our wedding that a twin was two-for-one, Paula and me. And now? Did we have only half a marriage left?

I could curl into a ball and wait till that interloper was gone. *Watch me do it. Or don't. That's the point.*

53

When we all came in from the cold, Artis finally emerged from the basement. We drank hot toddies and hot cocoa, but I could no longer feel the whiskey burn my sister's belly.

We were the last, again, to bed. Of course we couldn't sleep. Looking through the boxes of stuff, I found the mother-of-pearl pocketknife he had given us and the rabbit fur coats he had made, while Artis lost herself in her phone. Doing what? Even in plain sight I could no longer tell.

As she had the night before, Mom slept on the couch and gave us each a bedroom to share with our husband and son. We stomped off to sleep, or to pretend to sleep, each with a spouse awakening enough to spoon our naked backs, each with a child in a pile of comforters on the floor. I heard the sounds from my sister's room, mimicking those in my own.

"How cute!" we had said to each other when we first arrived, kissing our five-year-old nephews, complimenting their new haircuts and holiday outfits. But now, in bed, I saw we should have said, "How fragile. How tenuous."

I watched my son's belly rise and fall, wondering if someday he would run away, too, and not come back until my funeral. If our patriarch, with skin as thick as oak, could tumble so hard, what about us?

When my son exhaled, out came everything Dad would never teach him. How to jump-start a car. Skin a deer. Build a campfire. Swear in different languages. Fuck, I could barely do it in one.

When my son inhaled, in went his resentment of me. Hadn't I, hours earlier, snapped at him for walking around with his shoes untied? Hushed and shushed and shut him up too many times in his short life?

Now I was gasping for breath. Climbing on my husband, I pawed him awake, kissing, hissing, caressing, and finally crying out. A cry that mirrored my sister's down the hall.

At our animal squeals, our children awakened. "Mom, why are you on top of Dad?" they asked Artis and me. "Are you hurt?" and "What was that terrible sound?"

I rolled onto my side and covered up. "You were just dreaming," I said.

I could hear the boys fall back to sleep as they turned onto their bellies, pressing against the frayed brown carpet we had grown up tramping down. I could almost smell the dirty laundry we never picked up, the footed pajamas we wore even after our feet broke through, the cherry lip gloss fermented into the sickly sweet smell of adolescence.

We lay in the beds we had made for ourselves, holding our breath now, as if any noise could make the children scatter like deer. We uncoupled ourselves, reeling with grief and love. For the man who gave us life and, finally, with his death, broke

	us	
	in	
	two.	

Acknowledgments

My story "Half," which was the seed that grew into this novel, was published in the summer 2013 issue of *Pleaides*. An excerpt from this novel, called "Granny," appeared in the April 2015 issue of *Streetlight* magazine.

Many nonfiction books and articles helped inform my understanding of what it is like to be a twin, including Christa Paravanni's memoir *Her*.

Many novels with first-person plural narrators inspired my style, including *We the Animals* by Justin Torres, *The Virgin Suicides* by Jeffrey Eugenides, and *The Buddha in the Attic* by Julie Otsuka.

My gratitude is deep and wide and sky-high. This book took many years to write and revise and publish, and so many talented people suspended their disbelief that such an unusual little book could find its way into the big world. They gave so much of themselves to help me, and I am astonished at their insight and generosity.

I will list everyone (except my family) in chronological order, from when I started writing about these girls in short-story form in 2012.

My MFA mentors, especially Benjamin Percy, who, when I told him about my crazy idea of making two narrators speak in one voice, told me it would be hard but also made me believe I could pull it off. Jack Driscoll, who edited my sentences to make them sing and taught me how to edit my own work. And to all my fellow students in the Pacific University MFA Creative Writing Program.

The Key West Literary Seminar for choosing my story for its Cecelia Joyce Johnson Award.

Phong Nguyen, for publishing my story and choosing it for the Kinder Award.

Gail Hochman, for reading multiple drafts and believing in the value of innovative literary work.

The Virginia Center for the Creative Arts, Hambidge Creative Residency Program, and the Porches Writing Retreat for providing the time and space to work without interruption or distraction.

Bret Anthony Johnston and his workshop at the Virginia Quarterly Review Conference.

Christine Schutt and Allen Wier and their workshop at the Sewanee Summer Workshop.

Brilliant writer friends who agreed to read the entire manuscript in various versions, including one that read like linked stories and one set in a sci-fi near future: Hope Mills Voelkel, Artis Henderson, Pat Dobie, Leigh Camacho Rourks, Louise Marburg, and Deborah Reed. I am boundlessly lucky to have them all in my life, and I am grateful for their moral support and insight.

Kat Setzer, a talented freelance editor.

Friends who believed in this book even when I no longer did, including Mika Yamamoto and Christophe Carlier.

Bonnie Jo Campbell, the judge for the Association of Writers and Writing Programs Award Series for the Novel, who named my manuscript a finalist and who went above and beyond the duty of a judge.

Jesse Lee Kercheval and the other peer reviewers and board members at the University of Wisconsin Press, who read my work with such care and enthusiasm.

The wonderful staff at the University of Wisconsin Press, including Dennis Lloyd, Sheila McMahon, Jennifer Conn, Kaitlin Svabek, and Casey LaVela. I am grateful that they championed my work and made the publication process so smooth and easy. I could not have asked for a better press.

Heidi Bell. The term "copyeditor" is too small to convey the magic she performs. She makes books better.

Sheryl Johnston, the perfect publicist.

My daughter, an accomplished writer herself, who read a draft and helped me portray contemporary adolescence authentically.

My son, who is always willing to talk about my writing.

My brother, Louis Waldman, who is not my twin but might as well be. My close relationship with him growing up inspired me to try to imagine the upper limits of platonic intimacy. There is no one we share more with, it seems to me, than a sibling, and I'm lucky to have one who was my teacher, my father figure, my companion, and who is still my dear friend.

Most of all I would like to thank my husband, James. He is one of the smartest and most voracious readers I know. He is a numbers guy, but he believes in the value of art to feed our souls, and he believes in me. He makes my writing life possible, and he fills my days with joy that is high and wide and ocean-deep.